D1927768

Summer Nights

A One Night Stand Accidental Pregnancy Romance

Summer Break
Book 1

Chiquita Dennie

304 Publishing Company

For questions and comments about this book, please contact 304 Publishing at info@chiquitadennie. Visit the official website at www.chiquitadennie.com

Latest Releases

Series

<u>Struck in Love</u>

The Early Years-A Prequel Short Story
Ruthless:Antonio and Sabrina Book 1
Savage: Antonio and Sabrina Book 2
Beast: Antonio and Sabrina Book 3
Captivated By His Love:Janice and Carlo
Brutal: Antonio and Sabrina Booke 4
Redemption: Antonio and Sabrina Book 5

<u>Heart of Stone</u>

Broken, Book 1 (Emery & Jackson)
A Valentine's Day Short Book 1.5 Emery & Jackson
Rebirth, Book 2 (Jordan and Damon)
Reveal, Book 3 (Angela and Brent)
Bottoms Up Book 3.5 Jessica and Joseph Short
Renew, Book 4 (Jessica and Joseph)

<u>Cocky Billionaire Boys</u>

Cocky Catcher (Cocky Billionaire Boys Book 1)
Bossy Billionaire (Cocky Billionaire Boys Book 2)

The Fuertes Cartel

Stolen (The Fuertes Cartel Book 1)

Saved (The Fuertes Cartel Book 2)

Betrayed (The Fuertes Cartel Book 3)

Carrington Cartel

Torn: The Carrington Cartel Book 1

Claim: The Carrington Cartel Book 2

Something

Something Gained: A Romantic Comedy Book 1

Something Earned: A Romantic Comedy Book 2

Pierce Motors

Refuel: (Pierce Motors Book l)

Pressure: Pierce Motors Book 2)

Summer Break

Summer Nights: (Summer Break Book 1)

TN Seal Security

Aydin: Book 1

Nasir: Book 2

Nicco: Book 3

Standalones

Until Serena(HEA World Novel)

Temptation

She's All I Need

I Deserve His Love

Mutual Agreement

Scoring with Sadie

Exposed (A Bodyguard Novel)

Love Shorts:A Collection of Short Stories

Red Light District(A Fantasy Romance Short)

Author Inspiration

"Never allow anyone to steal your joy. It doesn't matter how many times someone says you can't do something. Invest in yourself—even if it's just writing down what your goals and plans are. Starting small can lead to bigger things."

—Chiquita Dennie

For questions and comments about this book, please contact 304 Publishing at info@chiquitadennie.com. Visit the official website at: www.chiquitadennie.com

Disclaimer

This work of fiction contains strong language and explicit sexual content and is only intended for mature readers.

This story may contain unconventional situations, language, and sexual encounters that may offend some readers.

If you're looking for sweet, fluffy romance, I would recommend another book.

This book is for mature readers (18+).

Introduction

Grab some wine and get ready for more spicy, sinful, sexy suspense!

Have you signed up for my newsletter?

Join today for all the latest new releases, contests, giveaways, sneak peeks, and more!

www.chiquitadennie.com

A Note From the Author

Thank you in advance for reading *Summer Nights!*

As a reminder, this book is a fast-paced novella.

If you are looking for full length novels, then please check out my catalogue.

—Chiquita Dennie

Jamaican Phrases

Baby Gyal- baby girl
Lowe mi- Leave me alone
Mi miss yuh-I miss you
Gwope- Stop talking foolish

Synopsis

A night of indulgence turns into a life of commitment when Venus learns she's pregnant...

Jahmir is a former player that never lets an opportunity for seduction pass him by. Working as a DJ at parties is something he enjoys—because this millionaire certainly doesn't need the paycheck! When he meets Venus at a party, Jahmir knows he'll claim her before the night is over.

Venus needs to get away and clear her mind after a bad breakup.

A holiday on the beach seems like the perfect remedy—until she is seduced by a millionaire! For one night, Venus forgets about reality and allows herself to be pleasured.

A one-night stand quickly becomes more than she bargained for when Venus learns she's pregnant with Jahmir's child.

Has Venus just made the biggest mistake of her life, or

can one hot summer night be the beginning of her happily ever after?

Chapter One

Venus

Every girl around the pool was twerking on whoever they could pull, while "Wild Thoughts" blasted from the speakers. As I sulked away with my third pineapple elixir, I thought about how that should have been my boyfriend and me. However, the asshole dumped me a week before we were supposed to go to Jamaica. I was so close to returning the tickets, but my best friend Isis told me to make it a self-care trip instead. Although I was having a great time, the breakup was still on my mind, so I scrolled through our old photos, deleting the good times we had. Those who cautioned me about sharing my relationships online were right, and I should have listened. The number of pictures I deleted of us together showed me that I was more in love than he was, and I felt like a complete idiot.

"Are you planning on nursing that drink all night?" The deep baritone voice made me choke on the last drop. My head whirled to the left, and what stared back at me caused my pussy to throb. I knew Jarvis, my ex, was gorgeous, and I never thought of any other man for me, but I was mesmerized by the tall, dark brown Adonis in front of me, with his tattooed arms, thick lips, and square jaw.

"Huh." I blinked repeatedly.

He pointed at pineapple drink I was holding, and my eyes locked in on his broad, long fingers that were perfectly clean and manicured. Hands and a smile on a man get me every time.

"I said, are you aiming at nursing that drink all night? You've been in the same spot for the last hour."

I glanced at the liquor in my hand and shrugged.

"Honestly, I was." I searched around for the waiter who had been checking on me.

My friend Isis suggested Montego Bay for the yearly beach party. I wasn't feeling it at first, but I let my guard down and got a drink or two.

"Interesting." My defenses were raised as he replied with a mischievous grin.

If he became a jerk, I wouldn't hold back in telling him what I thought, especially after dealing with a condescending asshole like Jarvis. "What do you mean by 'interesting'?"

Staring down at me with his arms crossed in front of him, he said, "It's fascinating how you're letting him control your emotions."

"What?" I side-eyed him.

"Tell me I'm wrong, and you're not drinking over a guy?"

I subtly touched my forehead and averted my gaze, hiding the fact that he had discovered my problem. "You're wrong." I waved off the waiter when he offered another drink. I fiddled with the pineapple. I rolled my eyes at the sexy guy, who laughed.

"You can let your guard down, sweetheart."

"Where is your girlfriend?" I looked around the party.

His smirk deepened as he chuckled. "I don't have one of those."

"You'll just tell me anything," I muttered under my breath as I sat up straight.

I pushed my drink forward, looking around at the people having fun.

"There is no reason for me to lie. Anyway, what's your favorite song if you're feeling up to dancing?"

The wind pushed against my bunched shoulders, making me feel cold. "Doubt you can control the music." Despite the crowd and trees moving in the wind, it felt like we were the only ones there.

"I have my ways."

"Then put on Beyonce's song 'Heated'." I tapped my cheek with a gentle touch.

He burst into laughter, and I couldn't help but chuckle at my response too. "He pissed you off badly," he muttered, putting his hands in his pockets.

"Broke up with me... but enough about my terrible ex. You've been keeping to yourself. You could have stayed in your room for that."

In my ear, he whispered, "You've been watching me, baby gyal... and besides, the DJ *has* to be here."

"Wait! You're the DJ for this party?" I asked, ignoring his comment about watching him.

He nods his head with a tight grin. "I am, and you are making me feel that I'm doing a terrible job. It hurts my feelings." He cups his chest, as if wounded.

"How so?" As he gazed at me, I tilted my head.

Those amused eyes swung my way. "Not once have you danced, and every guy who approached, you've dismissed—which I am happy about." He smirked at me and licked his lips.

"Why would that make you happy?" Gazing into his dark brown eyes, I realized I hadn't gotten his name. I took his hand when he extended it to me, the soft caress over my knuckles sent arousal to my pussy.

"Jahmir."

Grasping his hand, Jahmir looked longingly at me. "Venus." I cocked my head to the left.

Jahmir bit his top lip. "Nice to meet you, Venus."

"Yo Jah! The guests want to know if you can stay a little longer." Another guy approached us.

"Tell him I will only stick around if Venus stays."

Upon hearing his comment, my brows drew together in surprise. "Hold up. You can't tell him that."

"Why not?"

I pointed to the group of people surrounding us. "Because I am not the only one here, and I don't know you."

"I like what I see so far Venus, and you most definitely like what you see."

"What makes you think so?"

"Not once have you tried to pull your hand away." Our eyes locked in an intense stare.

I looked down at our attached hands and remembered that we weren't alone. "Don't you need to be doing your job?"

"My job is to ensure that all guests enjoy themselves." An alert on his phone interrupted him, but he ignored the call.

I had no clue why, but I had timed our interaction. "But you've been standing with me for the last twenty minutes."

"So does that mean I need to do more to entertain you, Venus?" He closed the distance between us as our hands fell.

"It depends on what the entertainment entails," I replied.

"My objective is to remind you I was here."

Flames of passion flickered in his gaze. "Don't you need to tell them if you're staying?"

"Give him an hour! Now it's all about you, sweetheart." The friend dashed away to speak with a guy I assumed had thrown the party.

Something in me made me feel like a schoolgirl again. "It's probably going to make all the women here hate me for taking you away."

"They will be fine, but you haven't answered my question."

"What question?"

"Do I get to have you for one hour?" Jahmir's tongue swept the fronts of his teeth.

I cleared my throat. "I thought you needed to focus on the party?"

He took out his phone from his pocket, texted someone, and then put it back. "All handled now. Will you let me entertain you for the last hour?"

My eyes darted from my best friends back to Jahmir. "On one condition."

"What's that?" His gaze soaked me in.

I decided to go the route of being spontaneous for once in my life and send a big "fuck you" to my ex-boyfriend. "So long as the condition includes you eating my pussy." Suddenly, I was covered in goosebumps. I was being direct. No turning back now.

"You can count on me for more than eating your

pussy. It will be as if you never had an ex after I'm done." Jahmir nudged me closer, his hands encircling my waist as he kissed me tenderly.

With ease, Jahmir walked us out of the party and down the sandy beach to a wide-open mansion. I was concerned that we were entering someone else's property. The sheer size of the home made my stomach churn in disbelief, as I had never known the DJ business afforded anything like it.

"Who lives here?" I didn't come on vacation to end up in jail. Is the dick worth jail? Observing him with curiosity, he whirled around to lift my chin. It's probably worth jail time.

"Me, come on."

I was speechless at the sight of the two-story Spanish-style mansion. It had an open deck that traveled down to the beach. I opened the door and strolled inside, shocked at a glass piano in the corner, artwork on the wall, massive ceilings, and wide windows. The color scheme of cream, gold, and white paired well with the art on the walls. I sauntered to a bedroom off the kitchen and shut the door behind us. For the first time, I felt nervous, like I was losing my virginity or something.

It took little effort on my part for Jahmir to draw me in with his eyes while biting down on his lip. When I told myself to step out of my comfort zone, I kissed him, and he allowed me to explore his mouth as well. As if I had too much power, Jahmir scooped me up with both hands and placed me on the bed, trailing kisses down my chest. Squirming beneath him, I could already tell he'd be the best lover I've ever had. Removing my clothes and then his own, Jahmir stared at my naked body in admiration. He took my nipple in his mouth and suckled, flicking his tongue over the hardened peak, as I squeezed my legs around his waist.

"Jahmir," I whimpered when his hand stroked my other breast.

"It tastes good, baby." Jahmir pulled back and slipped the condom on.

Ready for him to fuck me, I slid a hand down to grab his dick and my eyes bugged out at the length and thickness.

"It's too late to back out now. I promise it will be easy." He smirked. Before I could think of another distraction, he thrusted the fat tip of his dick in, taking my breath away.

"Ye-yeah, I've never been with someone this big," I stammered.

"Shit, warm and tight."

I already felt close to coming. It was embarrassing that a complete stranger could get me this carried away after only a few strokes. Coupled with my hatred for my ex, I needed to clear my head and enjoy what a one-night stand could be.

"Ohhh...my," I cooed, rolling my hips.

"Take what you want baby." Jahmir spread my legs wide, controlling my pace. My back arched off the bed, the sounds of our bodies moving in sync erupted around us. His loud groans and grunts made me smile.

Gripping my hands around his neck, he dropped his head down to the crook of my neck and thrusted faster. I cried out, feeling like I was floating on air.

"Right there, please keep going Jah!" I begged, head tossed and turned to capture his mouth.

"Fuck! You promise to give me this good shit again?"

I couldn't lie and say I would ever see him again—we

lived in two different worlds—but right now, the best orgasm of my life surrounded me, and nothing would stop me from getting there. "Yes! Baby whenever, wherever!" I screamed. My nectar drenched his sheets and stomach.

"Damn Venus. Pussy gonna make me crazy." He eased out of me. My breath caught in my throat as my head spun with confusion. There was an intense aura about him that left me on edge with a wide grin as he pushed back inside.

"Give me more."

"Open for me baby, let me enjoy you."

My eyes rolled into the back of my head as Jahmir grabbed hold of the headboard and circled his hips, giving me the best strokes in the world. Our tongues tangoed, and my heart pounded in my chest until I came back to Earth.

* * *

Early morning came. One-night stands can work for some people, but I couldn't shake the anxiety, so in the middle of the night, I'd slipped out and prayed that he would forget all about us.

Taking a deep breath, I listened to Isis yell at her boyfriend on the other end of the phone for putting his feet on the dining table.

"Okay girl, I'm back." Something he said caused her to giggle.

I whispered, "Isis, I slept with a stranger last night."

"How was it?" As usual Isis wanted the details of his sex game.

Darting my eyes around the restaurant to make sure no one heard me, I said, "That's not the point."

"Venus, you need to relax and enjoy the island."

Trying to hide, I slouched close to the table. "Well, it brought me...Oh, my God, he's here." Knots formed in my stomach.

Isis quipped, "Who?"

To avoid eye contact, I focused on my cup of coffee and added sugar with my spoon.

"Is he—" At the same moment Isis started speaking, my phone was removed and put on the table.

"Give me my phone," I calmly spoke.

"I never had a woman leave my bed in the middle of the night." Propping his arm against the chair back, Jahmir ended the call, his face unreadable.

I cleared my throat. Isis must have known something was wrong because she called back, and Jahmir answered.

"She's busy right now." Jahmir focused directly on me as he moistened his lips. As I rose from the seat, I leaned over to grab it. "She's trying to get her phone back, but her privileges are revoked." While Jahmir taunted, he put the phone on speaker, listening to Isis snickering.

"Isis seriously."

"Sorry friend, but he sounds sexy," Isis responded.

"All right that's enough. Goodbye Isis." Reaching for the phone, Jahmir moved it further away from me.

Jahmir said, "Isis, tell your friend, she's wrong for leaving me."

"Isis, if you say anything—" I glared at him, my features tight.

"Girl hush, my new friend told you what's up. Have fun and call me later." Isis rushed the call, and Jahmir slid the phone into his jacket pocket.

"I need my phone back."

He grinned. "Later."

"Jahmir." My brows drew into a scowl.

"Venus," he mocked.

I popped back down in the chair, folding my arms in a huff.

"You're cute when you frown," he teased, leaning forward, and the waitress approached.

"Hello, would you like the usual Jahmir?" she asked.

"Yeah, and whatever she wants is on me." Jahmir rubbed his hands together.

"I'm fine," I told her.

The waitress nodded and walked off, smiling at me.

"There's plenty of empty tables around here you can take." I gestured around the restaurant.

Tapping the top of the table, Jahmir declared, "I like this one."

"Why?"

"Due to your presence," Jahmir answered with a seductive grin.

"I think you got the wrong idea. Last night was nice, but it was a one-night stand."

"Are you sure?" His answer felt mocking.

I narrowed my eyes before answering. "Yes."

"Do you have one-night stands often?"

I gasped in shock. "Are you calling me a hoe?"

He waved his hand around in the air. "What? No, just asked to clarify."

The waitress approached with his food, acting like he was always with me at the table, refilling my coffee and leaving his drink.

"I should go." I stood, gathered my things, and started to leave.

"Where are you off to now?" The lingering scent of his cologne served as a reminder of the night before.

"My flight back home."

He cut into his food, taking his eyes off me. "Okay. It was nice meeting you, Venus."

"Um, it was nice meeting you, as well." With a slow rise from the booth, I blew out a gentle breath then headed towards the door. I was frustrated from being ignored, yet I set a boundary and calmly left toward the entrance door of the restaurant inside the hotel. I paused Looking back over my shoulder, and we met eyes.

Turning around, I closed my eyes with a deep sigh. "One night only Venus."

Chapter Two

Jahmir

Five Months Later

Stepping off my private jet, I removed my Gucci sunglasses and hopped into my Bentley. I had just returned from London and Paris, taking care of my business, and arranging meetings. Usually, I would immediately return from a business trip, but the day Venus left my restaurant, I received a call about an available property for a hotel in London, which I had been wanting to open for years. The only way to check it out was to go there, and it turned into me staying a little longer and traveling to Paris to go over a few updates with my team about my club, Hookup.

Even though Venus prided herself on it being a one-and-done thing, I thought the multiple orgasms would send a signal to stay a little longer and get to know each other. That morning at the restaurant, it was funny to see that she still hadn't caught on.

I owned the entire hotel, but money wasn't something I bragged about. I grew up in humble beginnings, with my father being the town handyman, and my mother being a housemaid for a family. Their struggle and determination to put me through school and give me a better life drove me to want better for us when I got older. Right now, I wanted to buy property in London for them. My goal was for them to never know about struggle again. I wanted them both to retire.

All they asked me about was having grandkids. I got my education, and throughout college, I became popular as a DJ, working every party. Now, at thirty, I could see what my parents had been talking about when they mentioned settling down, because two of my friends had kids and a wife.

Tonight was my best friend Dajuan's birthday party. He asked me to be the DJ—even though I already provided the club, booze, and food, as promised. Dajuan grew up with me and met my other friends, Lawrence and Brantly, from my business dealings.

Closing my car door, I waved to my driver, Glenroy, and reminded him to take the rest of the day off since I tended to handle things on my own when I was home. Occasionally, my chef and housekeeper, Jenny, came in, but I managed to cook and clean my own place the rest of the time.

Answering my ringing phone, I smiled at my mother's name popping up as usual. She always called when I got back into town. My parents had a property near mine on the beach.

Remembering the night that I brought Venus here and saw the sparkle in her eyes at seeing my home sent peace into my heart.

"Hello Mother." I opened the fridge and took out a bottle of water, easing against the counter.

"Happy to hear from you baby boy." Mother's thick Jamaican accent boasted loudly.

"What's going on with you?"

"Finished working in my garden and saw it was time for you to come home."

"Mother, you have an entire beach to hang out on. Father must be busy with his little band." I chuckled, reminding my mom of those restless nights when my father liked to play in his band on the weekends. I got my love of music watching him play drums on the weekends.

"*Gwope*," she huffed, asking me to stop my foolishness.

I laughed at her annoyance.

"Are you enjoying the new updates to the spa at the hotel?" Another reason I love being close to my parents is getting their opinion on my business acumen. Customer service is my highest priority and when they love something I implemented then I know I made the right choices.

"It was wonderful, Jahmir."

"Glad to hear and did you leave a review?"

She smacked her lips. "Now boy, who are you to be questioning me?"

I bent over in laughter hearing her go off on me. "Mother, I'm joking."

"Joke your way to get me some grandbabies."

"Honestly, I haven't met anyone that brings me happiness like you bring Father."

"What about the woman you told me about you a few months ago?"

Shrugging, I made my way from the kitchen to my main bedroom. Due to the memories, I stayed away from the guest bedroom, where I'd brought Venus. Unhooking my cufflinks, I slid out of my shoes. I grabbed a shirt, fresh briefs, and pants to head into the shower and relax before running down my day with my assistant. "She was a one-time thing."

"I never understand you kids nowadays with one and done."

"We can't all find our long-lasting love from a store trip."

My father had told me the story of meeting my mother when they bumped into each other one afternoon coming home from the store. He hadn't had enough money for something, and she offered to let him come to her house and have dinner with her family. From that day forth, Cedella and Ozzy Blackstone were glued together. Over thirty-three years of marriage looked beautiful on them.

"Love will surprise you. Are you coming for dinner tonight?"

Turning on the shower, I stood to pull a towel from the shelf. "I will try, but I need to check in with the staff and Dajuan's birthday is tonight."

"That means no, so you leave your mother hanging once again," she fussed, and I tried to hold in my laughter, but found it comical how she could use guilt trips.

"Mother, let me get through work first and if I have time I promise to call."

"No problem, but you'll miss out on your favorite."

"So, you think bribing me will work?"

"I am your mother. I don't bribe, little boy." She hung up before I could respond.

Shaking my head, I laid my phone on the counter, jumped in the shower, and lathered up my washcloth with my Calvin Klein body wash.

Forty minutes later, I locked up, hopped on my bike, and headed to the hotel less than five minutes away. I parked and took off my helmet, then was greeted by my valet. I handed my keys over so that he could park in a reserved space, and then tipped him, strolled into the lobby, and smiled at the ten-story luxury building. Blackstone Industries would become as much of a household name as Hilton, as I grew tourism in our town.

"Hi Boss." Alvita, my assistant, stood at the counter waiting for me. Alvita started in housecleaning and worked her way up to being my assistant after five years, and I treated her like the little sister I always wanted.

"Pipsqueak, how are you?"

"*Lowe mi.*" She frowned, wanting me to leave her alone, and flicked me off.

I pinched her cheek and she slapped it away. She handed me my normal green juice and trailed me to my office. "You miss me."

"Actually, I had a great five-month break," Alvita tittered.

I frowned, gulping my drink.

"Unlike you, I had work while I was away." I logged into my computer bringing up the plans for the London hotel.

"Dajuan and Lawrence have kept me aware of your work." Alvita rolled her eyes.

"Meaning?"

Alvita wagged her finger at me. "Surprised you don't have several women trying to move down here to claim you."

"Maybe I should have a brothel."

She gasped. "Shut your mouth, now."

"Still young, I can play the field."

"True and you can settle with a nice girl and stop running from anything that talks back to you," Alvita sassed.

Alvita knew I was a lover and affectionate and never had a problem with showering a woman with gifts, letting her know my intentions. My father taught me, even growing up with little money, the importance of showing your woman they're important to you. He showed by walking her home from work or sending her flowers, and even holding her while she cried when they lost a baby.

I sighed. "I hear you, Alvita."

"Glad you do, but to get back on the subject, Dajuan's party is ready."

"Are the girls ready?" I handpicked five girls to come into the club and do a little dance for him.

"Yes," Alvita hissed in irritation.

"Perfect. I liked the London location and sent an offer to my lawyer. I need you to draw up the formal announcement."

"What about the upgrades to the Paris club? You said to put a freeze until the budget was clear."

I calculated everything I had planned for the next few months. A few extra thousand would help me overall if I could pull off being in the London building.

"Stick to the budget and not a penny more. Tell Harper to send everything to the account and get my approval first."

"Great." Alvita started to leave.

"Alvita."

Her eyes lifted to mine. "Yes?"

"Great job managing the hotel while I was gone, proud of you, pipsqueak."

Alvita pushed her glasses on her face, smiled, bowed, and skipped out of my office. "You're welcome!"

* * *

Bob Marley played on the sound system, each girl dipped low and came up rolling their hips in Jamaican flag string bikinis that barely covered their breasts and pussies. Dajuan's face never wavered while he locked in on each woman, and I prayed that he would go straight home to his wife and not take a girl, because I couldn't be responsible for a grown man.

Clapping him on the shoulder, I joked, "My boy is mesmerized by Kotch." He nodded, never removing his eyes from the woman. I puffed on the cigar with Brantly chuckling next to me in the VIP booth.

"I told him to go rub one out in the bathroom. I think he's blinked once," Lawrence teased, puffing on his joint.

Drinks moved through the crowd and Dajuan finally came up for air when the music switched. I had my music assistant handle it. Even though I was DJ tonight, Bembe was pretentious with learning the business of becoming a DJ. The kid is only nineteen and in love with Alvita, but she barely noticed him.

Lawrence passed the joint to Dajuan and started shaking his shoulders, getting up to dance behind a girl.

Inside my hotel, I'd built a club called Paradise, and the sister club would be Hookup in London, the same as the one in Paris. Lights streamed down onto the floor, and the crowd screamed in excitement. Men lined up behind their women, and the vibes flowed. I loved what I did for a living.

"I will be back in a second."

"Where are you going?" Brantly pressed.

"To check on my business from my office. Keep having fun with the birthday boy." I exhaled and watched the couples hugging, kissing, and groping against the walls. It made me remember Venus, and how she melted in my arms during our time together.

Getting off the elevator, I stepped into my office, closed the door, and sat down to get a breather from the loud noise. Bembe had things under control with the music, so I could clear my head.

I cursed myself for forgetting to get Venus'number that night, and at the same time, I was pissed off that she disappeared—even on social media. I tried typing in her name, but nothing popped up. It felt like a ghost that had come in to disturb my mind, and once the goal was completed, it left behind a mark.

"Hello pretty lady," I said, answering the call from my mother as I gathered up my papers and put them in order.

"Jahmir Blackstone, I am still waiting," my mother responded.

Laughing at her anger, I scanned the crowd of people in the camera, noticing Alvita standing next to Bembe in the booth talking

"Father must have gone to bed."

"He could only stay up for so long, you know him." She laughed.

"He had a gig this weekend?"

"Yes, and I was shocked the place filled up quickly. I felt like I was a groupie."

I was taken aback, and my brow furrowed when she mentioned groupies. "What do you know about being a groupie?"

"Oh, pooh. Your father loves his band, and it brings

me joy to see him happy with a hobby, same as me with my garden. Now, get done and come see your parents before we are gone."

"Are you dying?"

"I could be—and you'd miss out on our last moments."

"All right Mom, the guilt trip worked, leaving the club now."

"Leave the bike at home." She hated it when I rode my bike, but I preferred it over my car—unless I had to bring things back and forth from the hotel to my house.

"I promise," I chuckled, ignored her comment, turned off the camera, and left to speak to my boys and let them know that they could keep having fun, but I was calling it a night. Bembe could work the last thirty minutes on his own.

Chapter Three

Venus

Placing my feet in the cold stirrups, images of throwing up early this morning filled my mind. The food I had at lunch came up as well, and my assistant had to help me clean up before a big meeting. I had to cancel at the last minute—even though I'd hoped to lock in some wedding business for the fall. Being a wedding and event planner came with a lot of responsibility, and I had a great team behind me.

"Doctor, please tell me I'm not dying," I begged, sitting up on my elbows to stare as she put on gloves.

Throwing her head back in laughter. "Relax and lay flat on your back, it only take a second, to confirm from the pregnancy test, and go through the exam."

"Why do I have to go through an exam? That test is wrong, nothing is going on in my world to be pregnant," I grumbled, covering my eyes with my arm.

"You can never be too careful, Venus."

"Jarvis and I haven't been intimate in months. Based on our last conversation, I would never sleep with him again."

"Mmmm...well."

"You may be wrong, after all." I poked my head up at the hesitation in her voice.

Turning the monitor off, she looked at me and said, "Seems like the test and the exam confirm the cause of your sickness."

"Should I drink ginger ale and call it a day?" There was a sense of denial in me.

Removing my feet from the stirrups and helping me sit up, she grinned at me. "Congrats."

"Congrats for...?"

"You're pregnant." Sliding off her gloves and tossing them in the trash, excitement danced in her eyes.

"Doctor, I can't be pregnant the last time I slept—"

Then it hit me, my night in Jamaica with the DJ.

* * *

I'm still in shock months after what the doctor had told me that day. I dragged a hand over my stomach and looked at Isis. "My feet keep swelling up."

"Well friend it happens when you sleep with a man and don't remember if you used a condom."

"Isis," I snapped.

"What?"

I rolled my eyes. "You are no help."

"Sorry."

"How am I going to fit in that little thing?" I pointed at the cab.

We were in Jamaica, and I came back with baggage I never planned to bring. My five-month-pregnant belly seemed to grow overnight after getting the news. Sometimes, I still threw up, depending on what I smelled.

For most of my life, I practiced safe sex; I had never gotten a parking ticket; I had paid my tidings in church. But one reckless act set me up to be someone's mother before I was ready.

The more I talked to my parents and friends, the better I felt about being a mom. It felt like a joke when I told Isis after the first doctors visit. She laughed and told me at least the best dick I ever got in my life really was memorable.

When I leaned on Isis, she instinctively grabbed my hand, aware of my sensitivity about my weight gain from the pregnancy. Every little thing made me cry.

"You act like you're a thousand pounds! The cab has space—and if you want, we can get a private car."

"No, that's too expensive."

"All right come on, we have to get this over with before your afternoon nap."

A chuckle escaped my lips as I threw my head back in laughter. Whenever I used to imagine pregnancy, I never thought it included falling asleep at the drop of a dime or constantly dealing with heartburn.

My parents loved the news, and at first, when they asked about the father, I wanted to avoid the conversation, but eventually, I confessed that it was a one-night stand. Dad was not happy at first, but he came around.

I was also trying to decide whether I should tell Jahmir. What if he rejected me? Or the baby? What if he was married with kids? So, I kept avoiding it and producing excuses. Then Isis forced me to realize that it wouldn't be fair to leave him out of the baby's life.

I didn't have social media personally, and my staff ran my business accounts. Isis tried looking him up with the little information I had, and we both came up empty.

"To the hotel we go!" Isis cheered, clapping her hands together, and I leaned my head back on the seat, closed my eyes, and talked to my baby boy. My parents and Isis came with me to find out the sex and when the doctor said it was a boy, I cried and felt it was a curse for the decision to not try harder to find Jahmir.

"Are you two vacationing here?" the cab driver wanted to know.

"I am and she's here to find her baby Daddy," Isis joked.

"Isis!" I barked. She hunched her shoulders, like nothing was wrong.

The cab driver laughed at her as our car turned out of the airport. "I hope you find him, young lady."

"Thanks," I mumbled, staring out the window.

"Sorry best friend, I forgot your sensitive ass will cry any minute."

I was distracted by my ringing Facetime call. I answered my mom and grandmother. "Hi, Mom."

"Hey Venus, are you safely there?" Mom asked like I was a teenager going on a first date. She sat at the table.

"We are."

"Glad to hear, your grandmother wanted to see you before you left, but time flew away," Mom said.

Waving at the camera, I said, "Hi Gran, I will be back in a week."

"Pregnancy looks great on you baby. Make sure you bring that fine boyfriend back with you," Gran responded, putting her entire face in the camera.

"He's not my man, Gran."

"Not yet," she teased, acting like an older Isis.

"Let her know Gran!" Isis snatched me by the wrist and turned the phone to her face, snapping her fingers.

Whenever I had them in a room together, my stomach cramped up so much from laughing at their antics.

After learning of my pregnancy, everybody was on high alert, spoiling me. My parents dropped off food often, and Gran knitted me blankets and clothes for the baby. Even my staff left gifts for me.

My child's life would be filled with love.

I grew up in a two-parent household filled with love, laughter, and a hustle mentality, as my mother worked as a judge, and Dad was a retired police officer.

"How much longer until you get to the hotel?" Mom pried, overshadowing the sounds of the radio.

I glanced out the window and saw us coming down the road to the Blackstone Hotel and Resort. I remembered my spectacular time swimming in the water, eating authentic Jamaican food, and gaining new moves on the dance floor. I could do a little twist of my hips, but a real popping ass was right in front of me whenever the ladies showed the kotch moves.

"I should be there in another ten minutes. Text you once I get settled."

"Remember to call us the moment you find the baby daddy," Mom joked.

Rolling my eyes, a warm blush filled my cheeks. "All right Mom, try to call you once we get settled. This baby is kicking."

"He must know his daddy is close," Granny teased. Isis cackled at her statement.

"Granny, come on, I thought you would be a little more conservative than your daughter."

"Oh no baby, you thought wrong," Granny replied, stepping out of the screen.

"Tell her Momma." Mom giggled.

I folded my arms and grumbled, "Time for me to find a new family to adopt me."

"My grandson will stay with me, you can go," she continued.

"See, now I know you're crazy. Goodbye Mother."

She laughed and hung up. I threw my phone in my purse as the car turned into the drop-off area by the front entrance. Isis stepped out as the driver helped me on the other side. I climbed out with my hips spread. Popping the trunk open to remove our luggage, I tipped him an extra one-hundred dollars for being prompt and safely driving us around.

Isis whistled to herself. "Venus, this hotel is a gorgeous girl," she remarked, sliding her purse on her shoulder. White and gold markings along the panels of the building were inscribed with the Blackstone name. A full waterfall in the front entrance with real fish swimming around and entire clear glass windows reminded me of Jahmir's home.

"Damn." The memory gave me a sweet feeling in my heart.

"Come on girl and stop daydreaming." Isis led the way in the hotel, our bags pushed behind us from the staff. I was a little tired from the drive and wanted to take a nap, but I needed to find out from the staff if they knew of Jahmir since he worked as the DJ that night.

"Hello, welcome to Blackstone Hotel and Resort."

"Hi, I have a reservation under Venus Kande." I lifted my ID and credit card out of my pocket to check in and smiled as Isis snapped a selfie of us."

"Perfect, I have you all checked in. If you need anything at all, please let me know," the desk attendant exclaimed.

"Actually, I wondered if you know a Jahmir, who worked as a DJ here once before."

When I brought up his name, she looked confused. It made me pause and wonder if she was someone he'd had a relationship with in the past—or now.

"Is there a problem?" Isis leaned her elbows on the counter, cocking her head to the right and stared at the woman.

Opening then closing her mouth, cleared her throat. "Uh, no problem, but may I ask what business you have with Jahmir."

We both jerked back in annoyance at her response. "Do you know Jahmir or not?" Isis asked.

"The only Jahmir I know—"

"Keysa, is there something wrong?" A young woman with black rimmed glasses and long braids came up to the counter and pinned her eyes on me, then Isis.

"Well, these two women are looking for Jahmir," the hotel worker answered and shoved my receipt across the counter.

The woman smiled and turned to me. "How can I help you?"

"Do you know Jahmir? If not, then can you point us in the direction of someone who can contact him?" Isis demanded, forcing a long breath out in a snarl.

"Unfortunately, I am the first person to handle any and all things concerning Jahmir."

"Are you his woman?" I don't know why the question came out like that, seeing as how we'd only slept together once.

She laughed, wiping tears from her eyes. *Was he that terrible of a guy?* I thought to myself.

Another staff member arrived and handed her a

folder. "Alvita, I have the responses from the survey of the last party for you to look over."

"Thanks, Bembe," Alvita answered.

"How are you doing, ladies?" Bembe stuck his hand out for me to take.

"Fine, thank you."

"How many fine men work here?" Isis inquired.

"Isis, I doubt your boyfriend will like you flirting with the hotel staff."

"Girl, please, if you found a Jahmir, then I can find one too."

All eyes turned on me, making me a little concerned about the man I slept with if his name brought on these weird looks of confusion and shock.

"What's your name?" Alvita questioned.

"Venus, and this is my best friend, Isis."

"Okay, do you two mind coming with me?" Alvita probed.

"Where?"

"Don't worry, my office is right around this corner. While that happens, I can have your luggage sent upstairs," Alvita explained.

"Um, I guess. All we wanted was Jahmir's last name and contact information. He still works as the DJ, right?"

Alvita suggested we take a seat, as she held open the door that led into a room right off the front desk.

"May I ask what you need from Jahmir?"

"That's kind of private."

"Yeah. Are you one of his hoes or something? Listen, we're not into anything kinky—and if you try to do something to my friend, I can and *will* hurt your little ass," Isis challenged, jumping out of her seat.

Alvita's eyes were filled with stunned amazement, and her hands were raised in surrender.

"You really have no clue what his last name is, do you?" She beamed, holding her phone.

"No, is he crazy or something? Oh lord. Isis, my baby daddy's a serial killer."

Alvita burst into laughter.

"At least you got some good memories. Is he in jail? They do conjugal visits out here?" Isis investigated.

"Alvita, do you have the latest reports from Bembe?" The door opened and my head whipped around at the familiar voice.

"Damn," Isis muttered under her breath.

"Venus," Jahmir said.

"Jahmir."

His eyes ran down my face, to my baby bump and a frown appeared.

"You're Jahmir? Well shit, you got a brother or something?" Isis quizzed, and Alvita snickered at her statement.

"Isis shut up." I placed a hand on my kicking stomach, my baby boy felt something going on, because he'd never been this active before.

"Are you pregnant?" Jahmir slipped his hand in his pockets, brows bunched together in question.

As I breathed in, my throat tightened. "Um, can we talk privately?"

Jahmir commanded, "Alvita, give us a minute."

"Yeah, Alvita, give us a minute." Isis sat back with her legs crossed and her hands in her lap.

My heart rate increased, and heat crept in. *Is this a heart attack?* I rubbed my chest. "Isis, can you go up to the room and order lunch for me?"

Isis moved to the edge of her seat. "Right now? When it's getting good?"

"Isis!"

Lifting her purse and phone, she stood. "Fine, but I'm calling your parents, this is too good."

"Should I have the housekeeper have food delivered for you here?" Alvita checked.

"No, I can eat in my room," I said.

Isis' lips creased into a thin line.

"She's talking about me," Jahmir answered.

"Oh."

"Jahmir Blackstone," Alvita added.

My chest tightened at the revelation.

"See, now, you have got to be kidding me. You own this place?" Isis whistled, taking stock of the hotel.

Nodding, he never took his eyes off me. "Blackstone Hotel and Resorts around the world is my business."

"I thought you were a DJ?"

Jahmir responded, "I am."

"He's a DJ and hotel owner," Alvita emphasized before walking out of the room. The room fell silent as Isis continued staring between us.

"Isis, you can go now."

"Right, I have to go to the room and order you lunch." Isis excitedly followed Alvita, swinging her hand in the air, and then gesturing suggestively. They handed her a keycard and she thanked the staff.

I shook my head and combed my fingers through my hair. "I had no idea you were the owner." I took a seat again, and he walked to the edge of his desk and leaned against it with his feet crossed in front of him.

"Normally, I keep that part of me from the women I meet."

"Why? Because you think they're only interested in your money?"

"Yes."

"Well, you have nothing to worry about with me. I have my own money."

"Good to know, so congrats on being pregnant." A hint of an attitude trailed his words.

I fidgeted with my hands. "Thanks... but about that night..."

Jahmir sighed, waiting for me to continue. "I knew what it was with us, Venus, even though you practically ran out of the restaurant the next morning." He chuckled.

His gaze sent heat to my pussy in remembrance of his tongue swiping my clit.

"You're going to be a father!" I blurted out, closed my eyes, and sucked in a breath, waiting to hear his reaction. Silence filled the room; I opened one eye, noticing a blank expression on his face.

"Say something."

Chapter Four

Jahmir

"Pregnant," I repeated, swiping a hand across my forehead. She was the only one I had sex with in the last five months. Unlike most men, sex is the last thing on my mind. Work keeps me busy, and so does traveling and doing exclusive parties as a DJ.

"Jahmir, look, I know it's crazy to drop in here and tell you something so important out of the blue. I understand if you don't want anything to do with him."

My eyes squinted at the last word she spoke. "Him?"

"A boy, I'm pregnant with a baby boy."

I dragged a hand to the back of my head. "Shit."

"If you want to get a DNA test and sign over your rights, I understand."

I swiped a hand down my face. "Wait, hold on."

"Being a parent is going to change your life, and I know women throw themselves at you and probably come with drama, but not me." Venus' words rushed out like *Speedy Gonzales*. She was forgetting to breathe.

"Did I say you threw yourself at me?"

"Well, no—"

My wrinkled brow matched hers. "Then I'd suggest not putting words in my mouth."

"Right, uh..."

"When did you find out?"

"A few weeks after I got back from vacation, I started feeling sick and throwing up." A pause followed as she tried to gauge my reaction.

When I got out of bed today, the last thing I figured would happen was me becoming a father. Circumstances were better for me now; the baby would never want for anything. The biggest concern would be us living in different places, what if the baby is sick and I couldn't get to them in time. I know I could travel, but being near to me and my family would make me feel better, I am captivated by her radiant, velvety, brown skin. Her plump, heart-shaped lips tenderly kissed my neck, and her expressive eyes revealed her power with each caress of my tongue on her clitoris.

I exhaled, taking a seat across from her. "I tried searching for you on social media."

Venus lowered her head and twiddled her fingers.

I calmed her by covering her hand. "I never had social media for personal use. My staff runs the business accounts. Overall, I'm not interested in showing every moment to the public."

"Understandable."

"So, where do we go from here?"

I slowly slid my hands in my pockets, hunched my shoulders, and stared into her eyes. "You tell me." I know she thought I was wondering if she was a gold digger, but it couldn't have been further from the truth. Alvita told me that I should have tried harder to find her, but I knew what had happened was a one-time thing and wasn't meant to be repeated.

"To be honest, I think for both our families we should do a DNA test to confirm, and from there, we can figure out how much you want to be in his life or you can sign over your rights."

If my parents heard her say *sign over my rights* it would give both of them a heart attack. Nothing about me says I'd be an absent father. I grew up in a loving home and expected when I met the right woman to get married and have kids.

"Do you want me to sign over my rights?"

"What! No. I know our situation is a little crazy."

"Again, you are thinking too hard and putting me in the category of your old dude. Let's get something straight right now; I am a man of my word. Never compare me to anyone. When the DNA test comes back, we can discuss how we will move forward together."

"You believe me."

"There's no reason not to, unless you're lying and trying to make me hate you," I grinned.

"Jahmir," she blushed.

I hopped up, took her by the hand to stand, and clipped her chin. "May I?" I bent down to her stomach.

"Sure. I wish Isis and my other family members would ask before rubbing my stomach." She poked her lip out at the comment. Chuckling at her frown, I extended a hand around her shoulder.

"Come on, *Mi miss yuh.*"

Gathering to leave Alvita's office, Venus stopped and turned to face me with her hands on my chest. "You own the hotel, so it includes the restaurant and everything?"

She asked and my head fell back in laughter at her stance of annoyance.

"That day in the restaurant with the waitress, she was being polite and probably thought I was crazy," she chastised herself.

I skimmed my hand over her belly. "I started the Hotel and Resort from the ground up, learning business and seeing my parents struggle to keep food on the table. I loved to DJ in college for extra money and both worked in my favor."

She snapped her fingers. "Wow! I never got your last name after we slept together."

I opened the door, hand on her lower back escorting her to the room when I decided to make a pit stop at the counter.

Out of instinct, I kept my hand on her elbow to keep her close. "Alvita upgrade their rooms to presidential suites for me," I directed, letting my entire team know she's an important guest at our establishment and to make her accommodations top tier.

Venus looked frightened. "No, that's not necessary."

"My choice."

"But we won't know for sure about things, and I'd hate to use you, Jahmir."

"Hey, I might be foolish, but something tells me that the little guy in there belongs to me—and that includes you... unless it's too much to have you stay in my home while we wait."

"Isis would be in heaven, but I think we need to keep things professional."

"*Professional?* Baby gyal, we passed being professional after the things we did together." I flicked my eyes over her curves; fuller breasts seemed to have sprouted since the last time we'd seen each other.

A familiar chime came up on my cell, letting me know it was a business emergency. She let out an exasperated breath. Alvita grinned at us and upgraded her booking to the top suite at our hotel. It might have been insane, but her being here was a sign that what we created from our time together could lead to a real foundation. No longer fighting my decision, I took her by the hand and grabbed the keycard to the suite. I led Venus to the exclusive elevator in the corner for our VIP clients. I watched her retrieve her phone and send a message to whom I assumed was her best friend.

I slid the keycard into the elevator, activating for the top floor. "Are you hungry?"

"I could eat, and I need a nap."

"Do you sleep a lot? I mean, has the pregnancy been good to you?"

Venus met my eyes. "For the first time, I'm not feeling nauseous, but my feet are a little swollen. My boy has been good to his momma."

"Have you thought of a name?"

"Isis wanted me to call him Vinny after me, but I declined, and my father has thrown his name around." I laughed.

We arrived at her floor, each suite having its own door for room service to deliver at their beck and call.

"Isis is on her way up."

After opening the door, I led her inside to look around and watched her astonishment at the two-level suite with the large windows, long, hanging drapes, private deck, and jacuzzi.

"Beautiful structure—and two levels, right?" Venus

inquired, running a hand on the gold tabletop near the fireplace.

"Yep. Because its my baby out of all the hotels I own, I try to keep it fresh and new whenever I can."

"I bet your parents are proud of you."

"They are, and that reminds me, we should organize a dinner for all of us to have a conversation."

The knock on the door notified someone was coming inside, which caused her to pause, and I went to help in her best friend. My staff brought their luggage from the other room.

"Venus! Oh my God, the presidential suite." Isis jumped up and down, enthusiasm echoed around the room.

"Thank Jahmir for the upgrade," Venus said, running a hand up and down her arms.

Isis turned to me with a big smile, running into my arms. "Brother-in-law! Thank you very much."

"Isis!" Venus grumbled.

We pulled back. Isis cocked her head. "Stop acting like you weren't happy to see him," she teased Venus. I could feel that her energy was fun and carefree. I hoped things would work out in my favor, and Venus'family would be like her best friend.

"Mr. Blackstone, I have one question," Isis said, shifting from one foot to the other.

"Go ahead."

"My bestie is no slouch, and she will be supported along with my nephew, so I have to ask; Are you committed to being a father if the test comes back proving you're the dad? Or do I need to have all my friends give you terrible reviews on Yelp for your business? I'm not above being petty."

"Oh God." A groan escaped Venus as she covered her forehead with her hand.

I held in my laughter and kept my composure, seeing the serious expression on her face. "I can promise, Isis, nothing will make me happier than being a father to my son."

Hesitantly, she reached out her hand and I caught it, shaking it gently and smiling "Venus, I like your baby's father."

"Would it have anything to do with our upgraded room?" Venus challenged.

"Most definitely and he's cute," Isis pointed out and I couldn't do anything except laugh at their banter.

"Ladies, I will leave you alone to relax before dinner."

"What dinner?"

I placed a reassuring touch on Venus' chin. "I'd like you to accompany me to my home for dinner so we can talk more."

"Do you think that's wise?"

"We can get the testing taken care of privately."

"Oh, right," Venus replied.

Isis chimed in, taking a bottle of champagne from the fridge. "Look at you. God, you must have a lot of pull to have a personal doctor come to your home."

"I do all right."

"Dinner works, say seven tonight?" Venus picked up her bag.

"Seven is perfect.

"See you tonight, Jahmir."

I winked and left their room to get the conversation with my parents over with before they heard about it through gossip.

* * *

I finished the call with one of my friends who owned a private clinic and worked with local testing centers for patients. After I put in the call, I made it my mission to come to my parents' home and relay the updates as a precaution.

I pushed my key in the door, knocking loudly to carry over the loud music. It was a normal day in the Blackstone home, with oxtails, curried goat, and rum cake wafting in the air, old-school music playing on the record player, and my parents acting like teenagers again, dancing in the kitchen. Clapping my hands, I turned the music down and smiled at the love my father was showing my mother.

"Son! Finally, you bring yourself home." Mom masked her complaint with a genuine smile, stretching her arms around me for a long hug.

I kissed her on the forehead, rubbed her back, and fell right into step with her five-five height at the kitchen counter.

"So, you *did* miss me." She pursed her lips. "You were gone for months and only called once a day."

"Leave him alone. Let the boy grow up," my father commanded, then joined us at the kitchen table.

Soon after making my first million dollars, I bought them a massive home for their retirement. At first, my father was hesitant, and it took many long conversations to get them to move from our old, 1000-square-foot brick home.

"He's my son," Mother countered, easing up to check on the food.

"Wait, I need to talk with you both."

She cupped my face, checking my forehead with the back of her hand. "Are you sick? Tell me what's wrong."

Grabbing both her hands I guided her to sit again. "No easy way to say this because it was a surprise to me."

"Please tell us, son," Father muttered.

"I might be having a son."

"Come again?" Mother jumped up from the chair.

"A woman I slept with a few months ago."

Mother waved her hand around. "You slept with a woman and got her pregnant, no marriage?"

"Let the boy speak," Father argued, throwing down his fork.

"He's talking crazy, we never raised him to lie with every woman and leave his seed."

I dropped my head in my hands and groaned. "Can we not talk about my sex life?"

Raising her head and knocking me on the back of my head, she chastised, "Your sex life is what got you in the mess now."

"The woman and I met five months ago. It was a one-time situation, and she told me today—"

"Wait! You only found out today? How do you know she wasn't sleeping with anyone else?"

"Mother, I believe her and Venus isn't the type of person to go around and lie."

"You believe it's your baby?" Father asked.

I released an agitated breath at the third degree. "Sounds crazy, but deep down, I do."

"Venus is her name?" Mother investigated.

"Yes, and she's here with her best friend. Unfortunately, we never got to exchange numbers, and she doesn't have social media."

"Venus should come for dinner and bring her friend.

How about her family?" Mother said, taking the empty plates from the counter to prepare dinner.

"Tonight, I planned on talking with her about the baby and getting the DNA testing done."

"Have them come here."

"It may be too soon for a family gathering, she's not from here."

"Never too early to meet my daughter in law," Mother exclaimed.

The fastest way to scare off Venus would be bringing up marriage, and my mother could get a little overexcited at the prospect of me bringing a girl home for dinner.

"We still need to talk a few things over before meeting the families."

"If you feel strongly that she's carrying your child, then we should meet her as soon as possible—I mean, unless you're not confident, son."

"Venus is special, and I'd rather not have her run off if she is pregnant with my son."

"A boy that acts like you." Her eyes lit up with joy.

I helped her set the table for dinner, sliding my jacket off and checking my phone for any updates.

"We need to all talk together. When are you doing the test?"

"Tonight, at my place. Khenan is coming over to handle it for me."

My parents peered at each other. I needed them to say what they were thinking.

"Call him to come here and we can meet Venus and get to know her better," Mother suggested, piling the food on the table.

"You're not letting it go, are you?"

"A potential child is involved, Jahmir. You sling your

little thing around Jamaica and expect nothing to come from sleeping around?" She threw her hands in the air and rolled her eyes.

My father sat there, trying to hold in his laughter. I slipped my hands in my pockets, wondering if I made a mistake by bringing up the dinner to my parents.

Chapter Five

Venus

Jahmir called me an hour earlier to confirm our dinner plans, but then dropped a bomb: His parents wanted to meet me. Even though I was completely sure that he was the father of my child, I initially declined and thought it would be uncomfortable. I preferred not to involve anyone else until the testing was done. Seizing the chance to meet his family, Isis wanted me to have the important conversation right away. I was grateful that she was there but unsure about how she'd react if they said something wrong. Whenever her friends were disrespected, Isis could become quite protective.

One last time, I checked my makeup in the mirror, then slammed the mirrored visor closed and smoothed out my dress. Jahmir had a car sent to pick us up. We'd gone to the spa and the beach, then had lunch on the terrace of our suite. Tonight, after dinner, we planned to watch a movie and relax after a full day of traveling.

"Remember to be polite, Isis. His family is just finding

out about the pregnancy, while mine has had more time to get used to the idea."

Laying on another coat of lipstick, Isis dumped it back in her purse, zipping it up. "I am more than capable of behaving myself."

"The lies, the lies, the lies!" I laughed when I saw the frown on her face.

Our driver stepped to her side first, then strolled around to help me out. Glenroy had worked for the Blackstones for the last four years, and he'd explained how they were normal and down-to-earth.

Sauntering up the stairs, I was amazed at the large five-car garage and modern stones on each side of the garden. The place wasn't as big as his home. Based on his upbringing, his parents weren't into the lavish lifestyle, and they didn't need the most expensive mansion.

The moment I pressed the doorbell, Jahmir opened the door, still looking amazing from earlier but without the business jacket, revealing a strong, chiseled body in a black shirt and slacks. It left me speechless. Jahmir gestured for us to come in and shut the door behind us. "How was the drive over?" A thrill ran through my body as he grabbed my hand and quickly pulled me into a hug, his arms automatically closing around me as I breathed in his cologne. It was the same scent as the night we had sex; crisp and not overpowering, with a deep bourbon-and-citrus top note. I felt drawn into his arms.

"Not bad, Glenroy was really nice," I explained, holding onto my breath. Felt like a teenager again, coming to the guy's house to meet his parents because we got caught having sex in my bedroom.

"Jahmir, your parents' house is beautiful," Isis

announced, handing him the bottle of wine we'd bought on the way there as a thank you.

"You didn't have to bring anything."

"My parents always taught us to bring a gift when we visit someone," I smiled, turning to follow him down the steps of the foyer into the living area. An older version of him and a woman stood together with smiles on their faces.

"Understood. I'll have to remember for next time. Venus, Isis, I would like to introduce you to my parents, Mr. and Mrs. Blackstone." Jahmir took me by the hand and led me around the couch.

"Hi, nice to meet you both, I know the circumstances aren't normal."

"Jahmir, you never said the woman looked like Halle Berry," his father flirted, causing me to giggle. I ran a hand over my belly, feeling a little kick in excitement from all the movement of today, and winced, taking a small breath to calm down.

"What's wrong?" Jahmir asked.

I laughed and shook my head. "My little guy is excited and kicking up a storm."

"Can I touch you?" Jahmir extended his palm toward my stomach.

"You don't have to keep asking." I grasped his hand, then placed mine on top.

Jahmir smiled, which made my heart swell with comfort. I'd done the right thing by letting him know about the baby.

Isis sat on the loveseat opposite me. Jahmir surprised me when he grasped my hand, helping me contain my nervousness.

"Jahmir explained your situation, and it did take us by

surprise. How do your parents feel about everything?" Mrs. Blackstone wondered.

Sighing, I clasped my hands in my lap and glanced at Isis, then Jahmir, before speaking. "Well, like I told Jahmir, at first, I had no clue I was pregnant. I only took a test when I started to get sick—and even then, I was in denial."

Suddenly the doorbell rang and Jahmir jumped up to answer. "After confirming with a doctor, I informed my parents. They've always wanted grandkids, but through the traditional route of me being married first. Once everything was out about meeting Jahmir here, they supported my decisions."

"Do you want to get married?" Mrs. Blackstone probed, shocking me with the question. Normally a mother hearing about her son having a baby on the way from someone who's not his wife causes chaos.

"I came here in the first place because of a bad breakup, so I won't do anything that will force me in a situation. I want real love one day."

"You're a beautiful girl, Venus. Any man would be lucky to have you," she replied, placing a hand on my shoulder.

Jahmir came back into the living room with a gentleman holding a black bag.

"Venus, this is my friend Newman who owns a clinic and is able to get the results faster." Jahmir stepped to the side, I started to get up and Newman gestured for me to stay seated.

Newman lowered himself to shake my hand. "Jahmir shocked me with the news, but he did not say how beautiful you are Venus."

Jahmir's face filled with jealousy as Newman complimented me, and I blushed deeply.

"Nice to meet you, Newman."

"I called you here to help me, not flirt with my woman," Jahmir argued with his nose scrunched up. The room got lighter from the brotherly bickering. They reminded me of Isis and myself.

His father jumped up. "I will grab you boys some beers. Ladies, what would you like?" Mr. Blackstone asked.

"Anything dark works for me," Isis said.

Everyone burst into laughter, as she stared straight at Newman. Jahmir was the sexiest man I had ever seen, but Newman's six-three height, wide shoulders, and bright smile gave him a run for his money—especially with his short, curly hair against his dark brown skin.

Jahmir took the test first, then I did. Newman stayed to have dinner with us. Mr. Blackstone passed me a glass of juice and passed Isis a bourbon, while the men drank beer. Listening to stories of Newman and Jahmir growing up sent flutters into my chest.

"What about your home life Venus?" Mrs. Blackstone questioned.

I finished my rice and wiped my mouth before answering, "Born and raised in North Carolina. My parents raised me with a lot of freedom, but they were stern at the same time, if that makes sense."

"Able to make decisions for yourself, but still set boundaries," Mrs. Blackstone replied, eating more curry from her plate. In the air, the smell of food lingered, reminding me of leftovers I wanted to bring back to the hotel for lunch tomorrow.

I cut into the dessert and moaned from the sweet

sensation on my tongue. "At first, I wanted Jahmir to know. Me telling him about the baby had nothing to do with money. I make a great salary, so money is the last thing I want from him."

"He told us you had no idea his last name is Blackstone," Newman chimed in, gulping his beer.

Nodding, I turned to Jahmir with a warm smile. He grasped my hand. "True. When I originally came here, we never exchanged numbers or last names. I thought he was just a DJ." I chuckled at my statement, and Jahmir shook his head.

"Glad to hear you're an established woman with a career. Jahmir knows we've always wanted him to be with someone who wanted him for him—and not for the money," Mrs. Blackstone emphasized. I hesitated to tell her that we weren't together.

"Remember we are not a couple having a baby together." Jahmir felt me tense up and tightened his hold on my leg.

"Why not? Is it correct that the baby is yours?" Mrs. Blackstone questioned, squared her shoulders, and drew the glass of wine to her lips.

Clearing my throat, I said, "Mrs. Blackstone, I wouldn't force a relationship to raise a baby together. Besides, we really don't know each other well enough to say we can make a relationship work."

"Back in my day, the man and woman stuck together if he got her pregnant. Marriage is the right thing to do," Mr. Blackstone remarked, looking from me to Jahmir.

Sensing that the night was going in the wrong direction, I started to regret coming back to Jamaica. Bringing drama to Jahmir's life and mine was not what I wanted. The only thing I wanted from him was for him to know our child, and if he was not on the same page, then I would understand. Both of us came from different worlds, and he lived in Jamaica full time, while I lived in the United States.

Jahmir blew out a breath, then sat back with an arm around my chair.

"Venus and I will decide what we want, but believe me when I say, I am happy," Jahmir answered.

* * *

Isis and Newman continued their conversation on the deck of the suite. Jahmir stood with his arms folded in the kitchen doorway. I placed the leftover food in the fridge, not sure how to start a conversation. During our first meeting on the beach, I hadn't been as nervous to talk to him, but now I felt like an awkward teenager, wondering who would make the first move.

Leaning against the counter, I tug my shoes off one by one, leaving them near the door of the bedroom, and remove my purse.

"How long are you going to be silent?" Jahmir challenged, with a smirk and a sparkle in his eyes.

A whirl of emotions started to change after he stretched his legs wide, and I saw his large muscles and full lips. From the doorway, he stalked forward and stepped in front of me, brushing a hand against my cheek.

He's teasing me.

"I'm taking it all in from tonight." Having him so close and the scent of his cologne had me in a trance.

Jahmir tugged on my hair, slowly running his fingers down my arm, then lifted my hand to kiss my palm.

"My parents liked you."

I shot him a scowl while squinting. "Did we sit at the same table?"

He chuckled, studying me with his piercing gaze. "Baby, I can promise you they liked you because *I* like you." He gave me a subtle wink.

"When will the results come back?"

"In a day or two."

"Okay, once that happens, we can make a plan to figure out the best co-parenting schedule that works for everyone."

Angling his body to stand on the side of me, he slipped his hands in his pocket. "Venus, are you afraid?"

"No, I know you're my son's father."

"Not that, I'm talking about being a parent? It's still new for me to wrap my mind around."

I cast my eyes to his face and smiled. "You have nothing to worry about. I can see you being one of those dads at the games, yelling at the coach if they don't let your son play."

We both burst into laughter. "I want to have lunch with you tomorrow—just the two of us," he announced.

"Okay."

"Newman will put a rush on the results, but I want us to really get to know each other."

"I agree, now that I know your last name."

"That reminds me, I have a trip to London in a few months to check out the status of my hotel."

"You will probably miss the birth."

"Unless you come with me."

"To London?"

"Yeah, we can set up shop there before it gets too late for you to travel... or you can stay here."

"Jahmir—"

Raising his hand, he interrupted, "Hear me out, money is not an issue, you can get to know me better and I can get to know you, plus once the baby comes, your parents can come here and meet my family."

"What about my work?"

"Aren't you the one who said you can do your job anywhere?"

"You're basically asking me to uproot my life, Jahmir."

Angling his head, he glanced down at me. "I'm requesting an opportunity to learn more about you, establish trust, and become acquainted with my son."

"Can I think about it first? My parents were expecting me back home in a week."

"If you want, then I can fly them out here to stay and travel when we go to London."

"Mr. Blackstone, I've made it clear your money holds no value for me," I grinned.

Our lips met. A weight seemed to press against my chest.

"Then hear my words, Venus Kande, you're going to be mine." Walking backwards, Jahmir left the kitchen. I tracked his physical movements as he exited and said goodbye to Isis. Newman planted a kiss on her cheek and waved to me.

"What's wrong with you?" Isis probed.

I bit my fingernail, planted a hand on my waist. "I think Jahmir wants more than a friendship with me."

"And is that a bad or good thing?"

"Honestly, I have no idea. A part of me wants to believe him, and the other part is saying he's like my ex. I have to keep focused on the baby." I exhaled, running a hand over the top of my stomach, exhausted from the day.

"Go to bed and rest. Don't overthink it, Venus." Isis stretched her legs out in front of her on the couch.

"We're going to lunch tomorrow."

"Good because Newman might become my new boo thang and I need you and Jahmir to be cool." Isis stuck out her tongue, turned around with her hands on her knees shaking her ass.

Shaking my head, I waved off her gimmicks. "Goodnight girl."

"Night friend!" Isis yelled from across the room.

Chapter Six

Jahmir

The sun sliced down the middle of my house, rays filtering through the curtains and caressing the wall of art I'd set up years ago. Today had worked out for me, because I'd had Alvita clear my schedule so that I could finally have the entire day free to hang out with Venus. The day before, we were originally supposed to meet up, but she fell ill and stayed in bed all day, stubbornly not allowing me to help her. Isis had argued with her to allow my assistant to help, because she wanted to have a date with Newman. Everyone at the hotel made her a priority, so nothing was off-limits, but Venus refused.

Now, she was finally coming to my place for lunch so that we could catch up with each other. Newman had gotten the results back, so we could open them together. I never doubted that the baby she was carrying was mine, but I needed to make her understand that I wanted more than to just be the father of her child. I wanted her to be mine.

"Sir, your guest is here," my housekeeper Jenny

informed me, escorting Venus inside. Whether it was the baby bump causing weight gain or the way her dress hugged her curves, particularly her plump ass, I couldn't resist being drawn to her.

"Thank you, Jenny."

"You didn't have to go through so much trouble for me." Venus' fingers glided over the tablecloth my mother handmade.

"Would you like a tour?"

"I would love that."

"We can skip that room, you should be very familiar with it from last time." I pointed at my guest room across the hall.

In a low voice, she murmured, "Extremely familiar."

"The place was built a few years ago and you know my parents live a few houses down." I took her by the hand, showing her the artwork on the wall in the hallway and my corner office, and went upstairs to the main bedroom.

"All of your artwork is amazing."

Placing a hand on her lower back, I showed her the wet bar in the alcove, the floor-to-ceiling plate-glass windows, the Spanish-style doors, the grandstand banisters, and the large, open space that combined the living and dining rooms. I finished by showing her the acres of land leading to the beach and deck.

"Gorgeous. How many women have succumbed to your charms on this tour?"

I raised a finger. "Only one."

"One?"

"You."

She pursed her lips. "Jahmir, please be real. You're telling me I am the only woman you brought here?" A familiar buzz ignited in my brain from her sweet perfume. Her stare challenged me.

Grabbing the fruity mocktail I created from my mom's recipe, I filled both our glasses. "Why would I lie to you, Venus?"

She bunched her shoulders. "Men do it for less."

I licked my lips, my gaze turned to hers. I saw her shift in her seat. "Are you scared of me, Venus?"

"Scared?"

"Of what we could become, outside of the baby."

"First establish paternity."

A lopsided grin fell on my lips. "Right here." I flipped the envelopment around and revealed the results. "Jahmir Blackstone is a 99% match."

"Congratulations."

"Thank you, now that that's done, have you thought about my suggestion on staying in Jamaica?"

Gulping down her drink, she put it back down, spreading her hands on the table. "I have and as you know I really am not one for being spontaneous, but I want to make an effort to connect to your son."

"I want more than a connection to my son. Can you give me a chance?"

"Be patient with me, still working through my trust issues."

"All I can ask for is a chance—but let me be clear, Venus." I stretched my hand out to cover her palm on top of the table.

"Yes?" The room fell silent.

"Never compare me to your former boyfriend. His actions only define his character, not mine." My voice became low and stern.

"I promise to give you a chance without any preconceived notions."

"Thank you, so tell me about yourself back in America."

"Most of my time is filled with family functions, work, and friends. You already know that Isis is my best friend. We've known each other for years." Her big brown eyes warmed at the statement.

"Do you see yourself traveling?"

"Traveling, yes. I want my life to be what I define and not how society says. Some days I work out of the office, others from home. I want to take my kids on trips while my husband stays home."

Her comment had me chuckling. "Your fine ass leaving me home alone." I held a hand to my chest in surprise.

Tittering at my comment, she covered her mouth, holding her stomach with hand. "Jahmir you're a mess."

"I call it like I see it, beautiful."

"Tell me about yourself. What type of women you date? How old are you?"

"Mostly, dating me is meeting up for dinner, and a casual thing. My work keeps me busy. I never apologize for building my business... and I'm thirty years old."

"I admire that about you... and I'm thirty-one."

"Taking care of my family and leaving a legacy for my kids is my only goal."

"Kids? Do you have something to tell me?"

"What? I want a fleet of kids."

It was cliché, but the way her eyes popped seemed like her whole life flashed before her eyes at my revelation. "Um, slow down, sir. One is enough—until he gets into preschool."

Letting out a guffaw that echoed throughout the room, Venus glared at me. "What is so funny?"

"Only person having my kids is you, and I can wait a year or two after my boy."

"Even if we're not together, you'd want me to have your children?"

"Yes, but I know the future. Favorite color and music?"

She held back her laughter. "How would it work if I'm married to someone else?"

I glared back at her. "Venus for your own peace of mind, we can ignore that question."

She counted on her hand. "My favorite color is purple, and I'm a '90s baby, so Jodeci and En Vogue." A burst of giggles stirred her belly. "Arrogant or Cocky?" she asked, rubbing her hands together in question.

"Confident in being the man you need and want by your side baby."

"Cocky," she muttered, and we both laughed at the same time.

"The food has me stuffed."

"Would you like to walk on the beach to work it off?"

"I would love to go to the beach."

"Where's Isis?"

"On a date with Newman, I'm surprised he didn't call you."

"We talked yesterday, and I got the results today, but he's been busy." I captured her hand to help her out of the chair. I gestured to the balcony, letting her step out first and leaving my staff to clean up the empty plates.

"Isis made plans to do all these different activities forgetting how pregnant I am."

We shuffled down the walkway, our feet hitting the

sand, the breeze all around us. Being in a great place financially had afforded me the right to keep my part of the beach blocked off from others.

Venus released my grip, bending down to touch the sand. "The beach is gorgeous at this time. Everything around here is breathtaking."

"I agree." I stared down at her flushed cheeks.

Wiping off her sand filled hands, she asked, "Back to you and the type of women you like."

"I go for independent, funny, sweet women, who understand that we're a team." There was so much I wanted to say... but scaring her off would only put a bigger strain on our potential relationship.

She admitted, "He cheated and got another girl pregnant."

A ball of anger jabbed my chest. "Your ex-boyfriend?"

"I had so many things planned out with him for the future, and one day, I got a call from his phone. He butt-dialed me, and I heard the conversation. When he got home, he confessed everything."

"Damn, I'm sorry you went through a situation where you feel like a wall needs to be up at all times Venus."

Sticking her feet in the water, she held her dress up to not get wet. Closing the space behind her, I slid my arms around her waist.

"Holding you accountable for his actions is wrong, but I do like you Jahmir, maybe a little too much."

I pressed a kiss to her cheek, behind her ear, and she placed a hand on my wrist. "Are we going to do this Venus?"

She turned her head around to face me with a slight, defiant smile, "If you protect my heart."

"Protect your heart, mind, and body." I began to cascade my hand from her chest, head, and hand.

"From the moment I saw you, I felt like my world was complete. You're beyond smart, funny, honest, and not interested in making me an afterthought."

"It won't be easy or perfect, but talking and getting to know you has shown me what type of woman you are."

She basked in the knowledge of her power. "More than the woman giving you a child."

"In addition to your irresistible smile, your soul, confidence, and strength are like pieces of a puzzle that keep me intrigued and wanting to know more."

"Then we're going to date and see where it goes between us." She whipped around, reaching her hands out to cup both sides of my face. I met her halfway in a kiss, gripping her ass cheeks. Venus squeezed her eyes shut as I slipped my tongue though her heart shaped lips.

"Baby, we better slow down before I have you spread out on the beach eating your pussy."

I pulled back, wiping the excess lipstick off my lips and grinning. Venus reached down and splashed the water at me, laughing.

"See, now you're in trouble," I grumbled, bending down to lift her in my arms and walking us back to the house.

"No! Put me down, Jah."

I paused at the nickname she'd given me. "Jah." I put her on her feet and tickled her around the waist.

"See, now, I have to pee because you tickled me, jerk. That's your new nickname—only I can call you that." An amused expression quirked up the side of her mouth as I studied her. Her voice was a sweet melody, dripping from her perfect lips like nectar from a flower.

After prancing around the beach for the last half hour, I was beat, but I wanted to show her more of my home. Taking her back inside, I motioned to the guest bathroom for her to freshen up in.

"Here's a towel and if you need anything, let me know."

"Thanks, where are we going next?"

"I wanted to take you to meet a few of my friends if that's okay."

"You want me to meet your friends? Are they guys or girls?"

"Guys...I promise the only women in my life are Alvita and my mother."

"I like Alvita and your mother has grown on me. At first, I thought she was ready to throw hands when she brought up marriage."

"Yeah, she's traditional like my father, but they've accepted my wishes."

"All right, give me five minutes to change."

"Give me a kiss first."

"Jahmir."

"What scaredy cat?"

"No one is scared of you."

"You know the minute my lips and hands get on you, a flood happens between those sweet thighs."

"Please, you're a little too cocky after a one-night stand." Venus blew me an air kiss, then shut the door in my face.

"I got your cocky right here!" I gripped my dick in my pants and heard her snickering on the other side.

I marched to my room to get changed and sent a text to my boys saying we'd be coming in half an hour.

Me: Make sure y'all on your best behavior.
Brantly: *Why?*
Lawrence: *His girl is coming.*
Me: *She is, and I expect you to behave.*
Brantly: *I'm a grown ass man.*
Dajuan: *LOL! In a little boy's body!*

I closed the message thread; they would go back and forth for hours. Once I was dressed and ready, I dug in my pocket to make sure I had my wallet, keys, and phone. I left my room and tapped on the door. Venus quickly yanked it open, and she looked even more sexy with her light yellow-and-peach dress.

"Ready to go?" I held out my hand for her to take.

"Yes, and do I look all right? The place we're going—is it fancy?"

Looking down at her clothes, she didn't need to change a thing. "You're perfect

"Please, nothing about me is perfect." She stood on her toes, sniffing my neck. "You smell good."

"Keep sniffing me and we won't leave."

"What if I want to stay?" She bit her bottom lip. I swallowed the urge to bend her over and fuck her after seeing the lust in her eyes. Tonight was about us connecting with each other, learning, and eventually growing into a relationship. Sex would confuse things if we rushed it...

But I might have to change my mind this one time.

"Come on, baby gyal, you're turning me into a schoolboy with a crush."

She drew her fists to her mouth and tittered at my pain. I walked her out to the car, helped her climb inside, and shook hands with my driver.

"Where are we going again?"

"My friend Brantly owns a lounge." Brantly had owned the place for a year, and when he wanted me to do gigs there, I never charged him because he sent customers to my hotel.

"Oh right."

My driver closed the door, put the car into drive, and left my private driveway.

"Today has been great, Jah, thank you again."

"Only the beginning, baby gyal." Brushing the creases from my jacket, I glanced out at the crowds hanging around the streets. I tucked an arm around Venus' waist. The closeness felt right... like home.

Chapter Seven

Venus

His hand found the brass-and-marble door of the slick lounge that Brantly owned. I knew he was watching the sway of my hips, and I made sure to give him a show. Jah captured my hand to keep me close. A few folks called his name in greeting. Staying close to his side, I saw the amount of people who loved him, and it made me smile. Jah had a heart of gold, and he had been respectful with my feelings since the moment we met. The crowd clapped and sang along to the music beating through the speakers. His friends were sitting at a table, and they clamored to make space for me.

"Brantly, Dajuan, and Lawrence, I'd like to meet Venus Kande."

I extended a hand to greet everybody, but they threw their arms out for a hug and I smirked at Jah pulling me close to not hug Brantly.

"Why can't I get a hug?" Brantly quizzed mischievously, rubbing his hands together.

"Baby, stay away from this guy. He's trying to live through me."

Brantly waved at him.

Dajuan's head wagged left to right with the music as he took a sip of his drink.

I was in stitches trying to hold back laughter when I saw Alvita rolling her eyes during their conversation, but I was glad to see her outside of work. Taking a seat at the end, I bent down to hug her. Jah spoke casually, catching up with his friends, temporarily putting business on hold while Alvita signaled the waitstaff to approach.

"What's good here?" I asked.

Alvita raised up her daquiri glass. "I love the grape and strawberry daquiris. They have nonalcoholic ones."

"Can I get one in the mocktail version?"

Behind me, Jah trailed a kiss on my shoulder and whispered in my ear. "Are you having fun?"

I looked back over my shoulder. "Yep, thank you for tonight."

"All I want is you having fun."

I grinned, snapping my fingers and dancing in my seat. His hand caressed over my stomach and down to my thigh.

"Miss Venus, we have to know what made you fall for the guy that has the worst poker record," Lawrence teased, tossing his shot back.

I leaned back against Jah's shoulder, staring in his eyes as he clipped my chin. "He's not bad."

"Ignore Lawrence and Brantly, they're both still trying to find themselves," Jah joked and the entire table rumbled in laughter. Our drinks got dropped off, I thanked the waitress, taking out a few dollars to tip her but Jah interrupted and put the money back in my purse.

"She's taken care of already."

"So, my money's no good here." I threw my wallet back in my purse.

He pecked me on the lips and grinned. "Nope."

The music blasted. I twirled around in my seat, ready to go to the dance floor. I hooked my arm with Jah's and nuzzled my head against his chest.

"Tired?"

"No. Can you dance?" I queried.

He grasped my hand and stood. Rising from my seat, I joined him on the dance floor. I threw my hands around his neck, snuggling close and moving along with the slow jams. Feeling his callused hands stroking up and down my back, I moaned. I felt tingling between my legs, and I was ready to relive our first night together. I slowly kissed along his neck. He lowered his head, finding my lips. We locked in step together, moving in sync. There was no more hiding my fears. Releasing all the anger from the past, I let myself enjoy the moment.

The music changed to a faster song. I stepped out of his hold, and we headed back to the table, listening to the crew joke and laugh.

"Dajuan's the only one married, correct?" I investigated, finishing the rest of my drink.

"According to Jahmir, you two will be next," Brantly threw out, making Jahmir shrug his shoulders.

"Jah and I are taking things slow."

"With the baby and meeting the parents, our boy only has eyes for you," Brantly responded, clinking glasses with Dajuan.

Watching them tease each other had become a normal routine that I found myself wanting to see every time we got together as a group.

Our fingers entwined in a loose grip, and I knew that I

wanted another night with him to find those same sparks we made the first time.

"Take me home," I whispered in his ear.

His lips curved, but he didn't release my hand. He just rose to help me leave the lounge.

* * *

Despite my obvious confidence from our first night together, I felt a little lost and scared with my baby bump in front of me and extra weight on my curves. All I wanted was to be close enough for his musky scent to make my head swim. Closing my eyes, I inhaled all the air I could before removing my dress in front of him. He stood less than a foot away, gazing from my feet up to my eyes. Under the dimmed lights, his charming smile appeared, and I felt more of his passion in that moment than I'd felt from any man I'd ever dated.

Jahmir curled one hand around my neck. "Once we take this step Venus, there's no going back. We're a family, baby."

I could feel my body heat up. Goosebumps prickled against my skin at his sweet touch. "A family."

"You, me, and our son Jahmir Jr.."

I smiled at the name he'd chosen. "Jahmir Blackstone Jr."

Stroking the curve of my neck, Jahmir captured my lips, slowly brushing kisses along my jaw, down my neck, and caressing my breasts. Throwing my head back, I fell into his warm hands, loving his closeness.

"Yes, Jah, please, never stop." I cupped my left breast and tweaked my own nipple. He walked me backwards to the bed, helped me scoot back onto it, and opened my legs. I watched him remove his shirt, pants, and shoes, then climb onto the bed and hover over my body. Jah trailed kisses down my thigh to my stomach, with magic in his lips. Wiggling underneath him, I couldn't control my heartbeat or my breathing, which was ragged and shallow from the overwhelming pleasure.

The palm of his hand smoothed over my belly. I cupped the back of his head, as he circled his hand over our sleeping son.

"He's going to be the best thing that happened to me, next to you."

Blinking my eyes. "How are you so sure?" I panted.

Seizing my lips in a quick motion, I latched my right leg around his waist, feeling him slowly pumping in and out. He cut off my next words.

"Because I knew from the moment we met, you and I were meant to be." Groaning, he buried his head in my neck, circling his hips. Feeding him my breasts, I couldn't stop my nectar from covering the sheets.

"You look fucking sexy pregnant, I want you forever," he announced, grazing my sensitive nipple with his teeth. It stung for a brief moment, before his tongue sensually took it away. He pushed inside me with a long stroke, and my thoughts got caught in my throat.

"Oh shit!" As I grasped his forehead to mine, I licked his soft lips and pressed my lips against his. If being here was ever a doubt, I had my answer now and knew we'd always be in a space of bliss letting the anger go to fight for the peace out of the pain.

"Pussy so crazy, I hate you took it away from me." His eyes rolled in the back of his head.

My pussy grew wetter at his statement. "I'm right here baby, stay with me."

"Ready to come for me baby?"

Snapping my eyes shut, I cried out, "Fuck me! Show me how much you want it, Jah."

"I want it all baby, can I fill you up? After we have our son, I want more babies." He said in the heat of the moment.

"Yes!" I cooed, feeling the bed rocking back and forth, our heavy breaths and skin slapping together filled the room.

"Come for me, Venus!" He roared, pushing my legs back.

"Coming, Jah! Oh, God, I want you... this... and our family."

"Give it to me, baby. Just like that, damn," Jah grunted, pushing into my soaking wet core, flicking his thumb against my nipple as we both came.

* * *

One Week Later

Jah never let a day go by without fucking me in some type of way. Like right now we'd been having sex for the last hour and his stamina was impressive and scary.

His ragged breaths fell near my ear, his chest lingered against my back, and sweat dripped down our bodies, flooding the sheets.

Squeezing my pussy tight, I grasped the back of his thigh. "I promise!"

Jah chuckled, pounding deep, not letting up while commanding my devotion. "No more watching without me."

"Okay, *Jah—*"

Isis and I both loved watching old clips of The Parkers together, and he caught us having the time of our lives. I had promised to wait for him before watching the episodes.

He rolled his hips like we were dancing, and I felt his balls smacking against me. "Come on my dick, baby gyal."

The ringing of his doorbell interrupted us. As we lay in bed catching our breath, he kissed my cheek, lips, and chest, then crawled out of bed and put on his robe.

I started to scoot out of bed, and he glared at me. "What are you doing?"

"Someone's at the door." A softening in his eyes followed my movements.

"So?"

"We can't stay in bed all day Jahmir."

Jahmir walked back over to bend down and peck me on the lips. "Says who?"

"Me, I'm hungry and Isis wants to hang out before she goes back home. We've been here for two weeks now."

"Actually, I have a surprise for you."

I sat up on my knees. "For me?"

"I wanted to take you on a shopping trip for you and the baby today."

"You don't have to do that Jahmir." The doorbell went off again. "I bet that's Isis."

"Go shower and change."

"What are you up to exactly?"

"You will see." He patted me on the butt, leaving the bedroom. I swung my legs off the bed to stand, heading to the bathroom for a quick shower. Turning on the shower head, I grabbed my favorite bodywash and cloth he picked up for me and got cleaned up. Coming down the hall after my shower I threw my hair in a high bun, hearing Isis,

Jahmir, and familiar voices talking. My eyes strained to focus on everything around me as I froze in shock, blinking back in disbelief.

"Isis I thought we'd meet at the hotel—" I clapped both hands over my mouth in surprise.

"Hi baby." My mom held out her arms for a hug.

"Mom, Dad. When did you get here?"

"Isis and Jahmir called us to surprise you."

My dad came beside us, wrapping his arms around us both. "Jahmir, really?" I asked, wiping the tears falling down my cheek.

"Everything I do is to make you happy. Are you happy?"

Nodding, I couldn't speak, in shock at having everyone I loved in the same room. "How is Granny doing?"

"She's fine and wants you to have a safe birth," Mom says, rubbing my back.

"I have another surprise," Jahmir confessed.

"Wait, not another one. My heart can't take all these surprises."

The entire room erupted in laughter. "Girl let a man love you." Isis shoulder bumped me gently, pulling me into a hug. Jahmir grasped my hand, leading us up the stairs and down the hall.

"Where are we going?"

"To the surprise, close your eyes," Jahmir said.

I hesitated for a second before allowing him to move forward. I watched all the grins form on everyone's faces. He approached a closed door that I knew had been locked a while, but I'd never had a chance to ask what was behind it. Turning to look at me, he motioned for me to cover my eyes.

Lifting both hands without a fight, I mumbled under my breath, "Annoying like Isis."

"Spoiled," Isis replied, and we simpered together.

"Thank you again Venus for coming into my life," Jahmir expressed. I released a breath, letting him ease me inside slowly so as not to trip and fall.

"Open your eyes."

Slowly blinking and scanning around the room, the same tears I had at seeing my family fell again from the baby's room displayed in front of me.

"Jahmir..." I whispered, feeling like he knew me before in a past life or something. Our baby's room was decorated in animal theme with giraffes, elephant paintings on the walls, plus the colors of Jamaica sprinkled around.

"When did you have time to set all of this up without me knowing?"

"I have my ways," Jahmir answered.

"Isis."

"Think of me as the fairy godmother," Isis replied.

"Thank you so much, Jahmir, and thank you for bringing my family here." I stood on my tiptoes, crushing my lips to his. I had to remember that my parents were in the room, and I pulled back before we could go for another round.

"He called us and asked what all you'd need, and we helped before we flew out." Mom let go of my father's hand and grabbed the teddy bear in the baby's crib.

"Jahmir Jr. will be here before you know it, Venus," Dad said.

"I know and that's the crazy part."

"Come on, I have breakfast being prepared, time for

you both to eat." Jahmir pressed a kiss to my forehead, escorting us out of the room.

"So impressed you kept a secret Isis," I teased, linking our arms together walking down the stairs.

"Baby, let me freshen up and meet you downstairs," Jahmir said, strolling to the bedroom.

I followed my parents downstairs. "Okay, hurry up before I eat everything. Your son is kicking up a storm." While roaming in the kitchen, I saw Jenny direct the staff to bring the food to the dining room. Picking up a piece of melon, I strolled back into the dining room and sat next to my mother.

"When did you guys get here?"

"Last night. Jahmir had a car bring us up and take us to the hotel," Mom exclaimed.

The chef put a plate of food in front of me, and I grabbed the orange juice, filling up my glass and gulping it down. I was thirsty after an early morning of Jahmir working to drain me of every last drop.

A snap of fingers pulled me out of a daze. "Huh?"

"Where did you go right now?" Isis checked, popping a piece of toast in her mouth.

I pushed a piece of pancake in the syrup and cut up the sausages, taking a bite. "Thinking how happy I am to have all you here, I need to call Granny and check on her later."

Dad was drinking a cup of coffee. "She's ready for her great-grandson to come." Dad put his cup down, adding more sugar.

Granny was the one I could lean on. Whenever my parents tried to be hard on me or not let me go anywhere, I would spill to Granny, and she'd get on my parents about it.

"I miss her so much."

"Jahmir said you are going with him to London, are you ready for the move, and the birth?" Mom wiped her mouth with the napkin, continuing to eat her breakfast.

"Finalized all the details, but he's done so much to make things easier on me, I think it wouldn't be fair to deny him more time with us."

"As long as you have your needs met, then we won't pressure you," Mom responded, reaching out to cover the top of my hand on the table.

"I appreciate the support. His parents have been amazing since I've been here."

"And his friends," Isis quipped, winking at me.

"Here she goes." Mom chortled at Isis and threw her napkin.

Everyone laughed and caught up, eager to hear about my pregnancy journey and staying updated on my appointments. I shared the status of my event work and the business being ran by an assistant while I'm here, then we finished breakfast and helped them bring in their bags.

Chapter Eight

Jahmir

"Are you sure it's okay for them to stay at your place baby? I know it might be weird to have so many people in your space." Venus laid her head on my shoulder as I carried the bags while walking through the shops. I tucked her close, kissing her on the side of her head, watching her meet the locals and get familiar. We'd already gone to three different stores. Isis asked Newman along, and I made plans to throw a little party with both our families afterwards. Inviting her parents could have gone the wrong way under other circumstances, but her father was cool when we talked on facetime. Isis had given me their number, and I'd even spoken with her grandmother and learned about their close bond.

I showed her the nursery. Thanks to help from Isis, her parents, and Alvita, I'd gotten everything done within a week. The great thing about having money was paying the staff overtime to get whatever I wanted done. Venus had no clue, because she'd been distracted with outings—either with my parents, me, or Isis—and by the time she came back to our home, it was late, and she would go to bed after showering and eating.

The setting summer sun was still baking the concrete rooftops in the distance, and I was basking in the relentless rays brushing against her skin. I splayed my hand on the back of her arm, helping her sit for a minute after walking a few blocks. "Ready to head back?" I inquired, dropping to my knees in front of her.

She fanned herself. I wiped some of the sweat off her brow. Shopping at the Rose Hall stores might have been a lot for her to take in after coming from the beach.

"I could use a little cool air."

"Another gift is waiting for you, if you're up for a little trip."

"Trip where?" She sighed.

"Do you trust me?"

Since being here, we only had the DNA testing with Newman. Getting her doctor to fly in had cost me a lot of money, but it was worth it to check on my son.

Sucking on her bottom lip, she said, "More surprises. What am I going to do with you?"

After helping her stand, we marched over to the waiting car and she climbed into the backseat. After throwing the bags in the trunk, her family hopped into the car with Newman and Isis and followed us to my parents' home.

My phone rang, Brantly was displayed on the screen so I answered it. "How's it going Brantly?"

"What's up with you?"

"Riding with Venus to grab my parents."

"Is fine Isis going to be there?" he inquired, knowing Newman was already with Isis.

"Playboy, you better worry about your own girl before she finds out."

Brantly grunted, and I listened to him complain about his staff not showing up on time. I let him ramble on until we made it to my parents' house. After finishing our conversation, I told him to stop by when he had time. My parents appeared at the door and started walking to the car to join us.

Soon, we reached our destination. Newman, Isis, and Mr. and Mrs. Kande all knew about the surprise, and I loved sharing all the different spots I grew up hanging out with my friends in.

"Welcome to Dunn's River Falls, Miss Kande," I said.

Venus' mouth was agape in shock.

"Where are we?"

"Dunn's River Falls, one of many tourist attractions. We won't be here long. I wanted to show you one of the places I liked to hang out in."

"Did you bring girls here?" Venus glared at me.

"Tell the truth," Mother taunted, getting involved.

I rubbed the back of my neck and smirked at them.

"Maybe once or twice when I was in my teen years."

"Well, going forward, you better bring only me," Venus huffed, gripping my hand stepping out of the car. Everyone watched the smile appear on her face at the location. I escorted her around, careful not to move too fast.

"It's beautiful out here."

"One of the places you can come and really relax and clear your head."

"When the baby is older, we can bring him."

"So, you plan on being with me for *many* summer days and nights, then?" Wrapping her arms around my waist, I pushed her hair behind her ear and stared into her eyes.

Our friends and family moved further into the water, as we stood back and watched. Since Venus was pregnant, I did not want anything to cause her any discomfort, so we only went far enough to stay safe. I'd paid to have the entire place for us, without any disturbances. Normally, the tourist lines were long.

"I wish I could get in the water."

"After he arrives, we can come back and take a dip."

"I would love that."

"The water is so blue! I think you've spoiled us, Jahmir!" Isis yelled from the rocks.

Turning with her back to my chest, I continued to rub a hand around her stomach, feeling connected to our son. "Newman, you heard her," Venus teased.

"She knows I got her," Newman commented, lifting Isis from the water.

Laughing at them playing in the water, my parents and hers stood off to the side talking and taking pictures together.

"You think they like each other?" I pointed at our parents.

"They better never get rid of me."

Groaning, I tapped her on the ass ready to be inside her again. "You make a decision about London?"

"Yes, and I can't wait to go with you."

"I have a place for us to stay and Isis agreed to come."

"I guess you thought of everything."

"The club is close to our place, so you won't be missing me for long, and Alvita is coming to keep me organized so I can be done with work at an early time each day."

"What about your DJ jobs?"

"I put a few on hold until after the baby is born. Alvita made sure to have Bembe step in if it's really needed."

"You're worldwide baby." She leaned her head on my chest, and I peppered kisses on the back of her neck. "Come on, my mom cooked dinner for us back at their place."

She yawned, and I knew she'd done a lot of running activities and was ready to relax.

"Ready for me to massage your feet."

"That's the best thing you've ever said to me." Venus wiggled her brows and grazed my chin with her fingertips. I whistled and cocked my head to tell everybody to start leaving.

* * *

Mom held a tray of drinks in her hand, passing one around the table. We were outside on their deck with a pile of food she'd cooked for tonight. Venus sat next to me on the bench, a dance troupe performed in front of us to end the night's celebration of having brought our families together. Venus curled up close to me watching some of my extended family laughing and joking around, even her granny called to talk with her. Rubbing out the tension in her foot, she moaned softly, and I knew those sounds would have me ready to take her to bed.

"Might be cliche, but I want to say thank you to Jahmir Blackstone. I'm very impressed." Venus interlocked her arm around mine.

"I like seeing a smile on your face." Isis approached the bench with a drink in her hand, Newman beside her.

Venus pushed her in the shoulder, a few people erupted in laughter. "What's going on with you two?"

"Mind the business that pays you. Are you going to DJ the music?" Isis sassed.

"Yep, Bembe is ready for a break by the way he's staring off at Alvita." We all glanced in the direction of him looking in her face as she yelled at him.

"Go save him baby," Venus chortled.

I glided a hand down the back of Venus' neck, pecked her lips, and whispered in her ear, "Be right back. You good?"

Whipping her head around fast and narrowing her eyes, she said, "Yes, I want to see you work your magic."

"Let me go save Bembe from Alvita." I stood, and placed her feet on top of the pillow, then jogged to the booth, removing the headphones.

"Bembe, go and have a drink, relax."

Alvita mouthed thank you, and Bembe sauntered away looking sad.

"He likes you."

"Too young," Alvita said, filming the crowd on her phone.

I changed the music to old-school reggae, getting everybody pumped up. Brantly and Newman stuck close together, laughing at Bembe. Isis sat next to Venus, watching the crowd.

* * *

A new day came. Popping my eyes open, I scanned the room and saw my baby at the door, closing her robe. Rising from the bed, I leaned toward the nightstand, checking the time.

"Morning."

"Morning, how long have you been up?"

"About an hour. Come downstairs. I cooked you breakfast."

"I have people to cook for you, Venus."

"I wanted to do something for you. After everything you've done during my time being here, I have to show my appreciation."

"Show your appreciation by staying in bed with me today."

Shaking her head, she strolled to the bed, reaching for my hand. "We have all day to fuck. My parents are leaving today, and I want us to spend some time together."

I stand from the bed, lifting her chin. "How about a change of plans?"

"Something tells me the change is me, ass up and face down."

Smashing our lips together, I turned her around to the bed, lowering her gently and removing her robe, filling my hands with her full breasts.

"Jah, you know that's my spot."

I fell to my knees, spreading her legs wide and pulling the strings of her nightgown down, flicking each nipple. Her back arched off the bed.

A soft gasp escaped her lips. "Okay, you win."

Chuckling at her giving in so easily, we made love all morning in bed, and then again in the bathroom. We ended up sending her parents out for a day of shopping with my parents so we could be alone.

Chapter Nine

Venus

A Few Months Later

"Keep breathing, Venus!" Jahmir rushed me to the hospital and called my parents.

"I think I peed on myself."

"Venus, you've never looked more beautiful," he encouraged, running a hand down my cheek. Even my doctor was able to phone in to check with the doctors here to make sure everything went as planned.

"How far apart are the contractions?" Jahmir asked, lifting and kissing my palm.

The nurse checked my vitals. "Two minutes apart, we're close."

I exhaled in small spurts, sweat dripping down my brows as I clenched Jahmir's hand.

After two hours of pushing, our beautiful, dark brown son arrived, looking exactly like his dad. Jahmir Jr.'s cries were the best thing in the world to hear.

* * *

I sat in the rental home in London, watching Jahmir, Alvita, and Isis, fight over who would get to hold baby Jahmir. The baby boy had slept through the night, but if he had started to fuss, then Jahmir would have gotten up to rock him back to sleep.

"How are you feeling about going back to work?" Jahmir queried.

"Good. I've let my team run things for so long, it feels good getting back in work mode."

Lingering kisses on my lips, Jahmir caressed my chin. "Let me know when you're ready to visit your family, we can fly out soon. I got things wrapped up here."

Glancing out the window at the rain falling, gave me a sense of peace and familiarity of home in North Carolina. As Isis change his diaper, I snickered at her struggling to keep a straight face after he peed on her.

"I want to go in a few days if that's okay, I miss Granny and want her to spend some time with the baby boy before we head to Jamaica again."

Sauntering over to the couch, Isis passed me the baby and I started to undo my shirt to breastfeed.

"Already moved a few meetings around with Alvita so we can travel together," Jahmir announced, making me feel supported.

"Can you believe we have a baby together?" I nuzzled my nose in his neck, loving the newborn smell of my son.

"Best part of you and me," Jahmir remarked, tugging Junior's feet.

"I ordered lunch for you two, and the plane will be ready the day after tomorrow," Alvita explained.

"Thanks Alvita," I responded, hearing a knock at the

door. Same as back in Jamaica, Jahmir preferred to have his own private chef and staff whenever he travels. A cart of food and Jenny with bags of groceries poured through the loft.

"We can eat in our room if you want." Jahmir jumped from the chair, greeting his chef.

"Here is fine." I removed Junior from my breast, lifted him onto my shoulder, and patted his back to burp him. With him squirming in my arms, I wiped his mouth clean. I strolled to his baby bed to lay him down for a nap.

* * *

"Venus! Venus!" Granny called my name, bringing me out of my dazed memory.

"Yeah, Granny."

"Are you all right?" Granny held onto Jahmir Jr.

I dragged a hand through my hair. "Fine, thinking about our trip to London."

"Or you are thinking about that man of yours and when you can have sex," Granny joked.

My parents came to my granny's house when I got into town, and they'll be here for a few days before going back home. I will fly back to Jamaica for a while until I'm ready to come back here full time.

"Granny, you're always getting in my business," I jested, leaning against her arm on the couch. We'd come to visit early this morning, ate breakfast, and chilled like old times. "He's so precious, looking like his daddy. Spitting image."

"Jahmir's parents said the same thing."

"You haven't stayed in one place for long, are you okay with that?"

I crossed one leg on top of the other. "I have to admit: At first, I only wanted to visit him for a week and let him know about the baby, but we got closer, and I decided to follow him to London."

"As long as he keeps you secure and supported, I can see a good change in you. More relaxed." Granny cuddled up close to me.

"Mom said the same thing, talking about how I have an air about me."

"Good dick, good food, and a nice smile will cure everything," Granny teased.

Raising my hand to my mouth in shock, my head swung left to right to see if anyone else heard her. "Granny really."

She tapped my knee. "Honey, I was young once, I understand."

"Well, the fewer details, the better. Are you okay with the baby? I need to go in and check on a few things at work."

"Go, girl—and hurry up, because this cute little thing will need his momma soon!" Granny released the bib he had drooled on, sitting him up for me to kiss him on the head. His little curls smelled like cotton candy.

"I won't be gone for more than an hour or so. Jahmir is here with my parents."

"Child, I helped raise you. Go away."

"Fine, let me leave before I sit back down and smother kisses all over him." Throwing my purse on my shoulder, I let my parents, then Jahmir know I was leaving. I hopped in the car with Isis driving to my office.

Checking my makeup, I removed my lipstick and reapplied. I twisted in my seat to the beat of the old-school music.

"How much you want to bet you won't be here long?" Isis cackled, turning down the street and stepping on the gas to head onto the freeway.

My office wasn't far; I was less than ten minutes from my grandmother and parents. She stopped at a light, turning down the radio.

"Ready to get back to my man and baby."

Isis leaned back against the door, staring at me. "When are you two getting married?"

"Marriage... Isis."

The light turned green, and she moved through it. She whipped into the parking lot of my one-story building, turning off the car.

"He's ready to give you his last name."

"I'm not rushing anything. I had a baby. We're still dating, and I like where we are."

Opening the door, I waved at a few of my employees. My secretary ended her call and got up with a vase full of flowers in her hand.

"Welcome back boss lady."

"Adell, you didn't have to get me flowers."

"Well, actually these aren't from me." Adell chuckled, stretching the vase out to me. I took them out of her hand, sauntering to my office to take a seat. Isis and Adell came in and shut the door.

Hoisting the card out, I opened it and read the familiar words: *You and me forever. Come home soon, baby gyal.*

"Who are they from?" Adell asked.

"By the grin on her face, I can only guess one person. Jahmir," Isis announced with a devilish smirk, placing them on the table. I sat back in my seat looking around the office I hadn't been in for a few months.

Logging onto my computer, I placed my purse on the desk. I got comfortable and ready to catch up on my accounts.

"Adell, how are things around the office?"

"Smooth, as usual. You know that everybody wanted to throw you a baby shower, but with you being in London, it wouldn't work." Adell gathered her notepad.

Sighing, I clasped my hands together in my lap. "Life is crazy busy for me, but I wanted to check on things because I will be going back to Jamaica soon."

Tossing her head from Isis to me, Adell asked, "Are you thinking of closing the office?"

"No, the last thing on my mind is closing my office, I can still work from home."

"Home. Jamaica is home now," Adell teased.

"One of many homes yes."

"That ex is probably pissed at those social media posts of you and Jahmir together." Adell mentioned that Isis posted of us from our time in London.

"He's the last thing on my mind. Anyway, the numbers look good. Any complaints?" I searched her eyes for any hesitation.

Adell flipped her notepad open, reading off the updates. She ordered us coffee from the shop around the corner. I set up appointments on Zoom with new clients who wanted to work with me. What was supposed to be a one-hour meeting lasted over four, glad I left breastmilk and I couldn't wait to get back to my child and boyfriend.

* * *

My father and Jahmir marched into the kitchen from the backyard holding a tray of ribs and corn on the cob.

Jahmir winked at me, then washed his hands. After strolling to the bathroom, I grabbed the door to open.

"Work was good?" Jahmir pinned me against the wall.

"You look like you belong here in North Carolina." I puckered my lips for a kiss. I brushed a hand up his back and pulled him close to my chest.

"Maybe I do."

"Possibly, but how was my baby?"

"Great, slept through and just got up a few minutes before you got here." Jahmir clasped our hands leading me to the bedroom.

"Where are you going?"

"To see our son. What did you think I was going to do?" Jahmir scanned my eyes, removing his grip.

"Knowing you Jah, you probably wanted a quickie," I tittered, opening the door and peaking my head in to see Junior lying in the crib sleeping.

Jahmir gripped my ass, and I felt his thick shaft wake up. I knew bringing up a quickie would get him excited. He moved his hand along my thigh and up my stomach. I saw his neatly shaved beard and thick brows while he stared down at me.

"Come on, let him sleep and come eat."

"It does smell good."

"Your father showed me his secret sauce, I think you're stuck with me now." Jahmir traced a finger down my cheek.

"Happy to be stuck with you, Mr. Blackstone."

Epilogue

Venus

A few years later

Staring at the sun shining over the beach, I marveled at my new life and felt grateful for sticking to what made me and my child happy. Even years later I was amazed at my transformation of not living life by the rules. The hurt and pain from the last relationship has never creeped into my head and I have my husband to thank for the glow in my cheeks. Smiling down at the large hands caressing my six-month pregnant belly, I laid my head back on his chest, watching the sun rise over the beach. Jahmir kissed the side of my cheek, whispering sweet memories of our night together when our son went to bed.

"Good morning, beautiful."

"Morning baby." I extended my hand up to cup the side of his face and turned my head for a kiss on the lips.

"Keep kissing me right now, and my dick is going to

poke something." He groaned, gliding a hand to hold my chin in place, sinking his tongue in my mouth.

"We better hold off because a little guy is going to burst in the door soon to wake us up."

"I locked the door."

I gasped and fell into a simper. "You did not lock my baby out of our room."

"Baby, sometimes Daddy needs a little alone time with you."

"Awe, you are jealous of your son."

He nodded. "Hell yeah, that boy hates to share you and when my princess comes, you're gonna feel the same way."

"You might be right, but maybe we can make up for lost time tonight when we send him with your parents."

He licked his lips. "Now you're talking."

Jahmir Jr. is the spitting image of his father and I hoped he would find love and happiness with someone the way I did with his father.

"Come on, I have breakfast ready."

"On the patio?" I watched him slide the door open, grasping my palm to help me on the deck of our home.

Jahmir raised my palm to kiss the back. "You seem surprised, I thought you knew about me baby."

Jahmir still worked doing some DJ gigs around the island, and slowly transitioned from full time to part time with his hotel business. A few times a year, he traveled around the world to check on his businesses, but eighty percent of the time he'd been able to handle meetings virtually. I worked part time while being a mom. Our new baby coming in a few months will take up more of our time and I planned on hiring a nanny for when his parents can't watch the kids.

All the grandparents loved it when we sent Little Jah to visit. Our baby boy was spoiled rotten, from his parents, mine, and my best friend. They added a playroom in the house that we renovated on the property. Hearing rapid, fast knocks, Jahmir poured orange juice in my glass, then stood to stroll back inside and unlock the door. Stepping aside to greet our son, Jahmir hoisted him up and kissed the side of his face.

"Did you have a good sleep, son?"

"Yes, why was the door locked?" Little Jah questioned, scanning the room wearing his Back Panther pajamas.

"Momma needed a little extra rest," Jahmir explained.

He put him down on the floor and Junior walked out to the patio, trying to climb in the chair next to me.

"Morning baby." I palmed the top of his head.

"Morning, Mommy. I'm hungry," Little Jah said.

"Daddy has everything from pancakes and eggs to donuts and French toast to eat," I answered, raising the spatula to help fill the empty plate in front of him. When I finished making his plate, Jahmir smiled at him and watched the waves come in and out.

"What are we doing today?" I wondered.

"The day should be pretty breezy, maybe a barbeque grilling, just the three of us with a movie sounds good," Jahmir replied.

I stuffed eggs with sausage into my mouth and moaned. "We could barbecue and invite your parents over."

Jahmir drank his juice. "A little party would be nice, have a few friends, what do you think?"

"Sounds good to me and I can get the chef to grab some groceries before they pack up."

"Daddy, what's grilling?" Little Jah asked.

"A party where family comes together and we hangout and eat a lot of good food." Jahmir ate his sandwich.

Watching the interaction between father and son filled my heart with so much emotion and I regretted not telling him sooner about the baby. I will have that in the back of my mind until I die; scared of not speaking up sooner and feeling like we would be a burden to him.

I wiped my mouth free of crumbs, and rose from the chair. I helped Little Jah finish up, then we headed down to the beach. I was still in my shorts and large sleepshirt. I had to get used to Jahmir's wealth, and how nothing made him happier than showering us with gifts.

Dipping my feet in the water, I laughed at Little Jah, running to catch Jahmir.

"Be careful you guys."

"I will be, Mommy." Little Jah caught his dad, and they fell onto the sand in a fit of laughter. The two of them could go on for hours.

I kicked my feet in the water, feeling my baby kicking in my stomach.

"Little girl, stop sitting on my bladder," I joked, raking a hand over my stomach.

Hours later, the grill was going, music blasting with Jahmir teaching his son how to change a song. I smiled at the interaction, taking a picture on my phone of the embrace when he kissed him on the forehead. Our chef decided to come back and manage the grill. Jahmir's mother made some of her special sauce for the burgers and helped set up the food table for us so I wouldn't have to stress. I gulped on the apple cider and did a little two step with my friends, wishing for more days like these.

Coming down from the DJ booth, Jahmir wrapped both arms around me, tugged me close, lifted my chin, and stared into my eyes.

"We have a whole lifetime to enjoy these moments."

Nodding, I sighed in relief. "Everything I wanted has come true. I'm glad I took that trip alone that day."

"I think our souls are connected and we would have found each other."

"You believe that? Soulmates."

"Soulmates, lovers, and friends. My life is right because you gave me a chance to love you properly."

"I'm so happy with you." I pulled him close and smashed our lips together, ready to take him into the house for another round.

"All right, you two, we have kids present," my bestie teased, holding Little Jah in her arms.

Jahmir reached for our son, tucking him close, while the music blasted around us, alongside the lively conversation about throwing a baby shower soon.

"Are you glad you listened to me?"

I frowned, jerking my head back. "About what?"

"Because of me you got a happy ending. The new baby should be named after me."

I squeezed her close, leaning my head on her shoulder. "Next is your turn."

"Men are the least of my worries."

"I recall saying the exact thing when I tried to leave, and you threatened me."

She waved me off. "I call it 'helping you find some good dick'." She burst into laughter.

I held my hands in prayer, muttering, "Thank you."

* * *

I hope you enjoyed Venus and Jahmir's story. Check the sneak peek of *Endless Summer* on the next page.

Follow my standalone opposites attract, age gap, military romance *Exposed* https://books2read.com/u/bQyYZe.

Are you a fan of sports romance? Then download one-night stand billionaire romance *Refuel* https://books2read.com/u/boDyDA.

Also, follow it up with workplace sports romance *Pressure* https://books2read.com/u/3Ly1r7.

If you love romantic comedy, fake relationships, and enemies to lovers, find it here in *Something Gained*. Click the link here https://books2read.com/u/baGLYy. Then check into *Something Earned: A Friends to Lovers* Romantic Comedy here:https://books2read.com/u/3JLRxA

My love of friends finding love started with the Heart of Stone series that includes a host of characters and family. *Broken: Emery and Jackson* (*Book 1*), a sports one-night stand workplace romance is here: https://books2read.com/u/3LoelX.

Then you can continue with a fun side story of Emery and Jackson with a Valentine's Day short here: https://books2read.com/u/4jAypY.

Jordan, her best friend's story continues in *Rebirth* (*Book 2*), a single dad, widow billionaire romance here: https://books2read.com/u/ba2OMx.

Please also check out a second-chance workplace romance here: *Renew* (*Book 4*) at https://books2read.com/u/4NXyPG with a host of characters intertwined.

Follow Desiree and Gabriel in *Temptation*, a standalone contemporary, sports, curvy girl romance. Check it out here https://books2read.com/u/mle1Vv.

Check out dark mafia romance here that started my journey with Antonio and Sabrina in *Ruthless* (*Book 1*): https://books2read.com/u/4AxKLo.

The relationship continues in *Savage* (*Book* 2) as they get to know each other and their families, https://books2read.com/u/bpED6g.

Antonio and Sabrina have more work to do in *Beast* (*Book* 3) right here: https://books2read.-com/links/ubl/4AxKOd.

Did you know Janice and Carlo have a book? Well, grab this dark mafia romance with emotional scars and betrayal right here: https://books2read.com/u/b6je6M.

Any fans of forbidden political romance should check out *Mutual Agreement*, a steamy romance, here: https://books2read.com/u/mgzzWX

Grab the full novel of Aydin here click the link here. https://books2read.com/u/mBwaOy continue into more military romance with Nasir:TN Seal Security book 2 a damsel in distress, actress romantic suspense here:https://books2read.com/u/3Ln7Ee Afterwards follow *Nicco in book 3 TN Seal Security* a fake dating, bodyguard romance here:https://books2read.com/u/4DDn7k

Have you checked out *She's All I Need?* Click here https://books2read.com/u/49lkeW for a sports, opposites attract romance.

What about dark romance that has everything from steamy romance, opposites attract, suspense, thriller, celebrity, and more in *Stolen* (*Book 1*) at https://books2read.com/u/mvZlgV.

Don't miss the follow-up, Joaquin and Sofia's story, in *Saved* (*Book* 2): https://books2read.com/u/4DWwLd.

The conclusion for Joaquin and Sofia comes full

circle in *Betrayed* here: https://books2read.-com/u/4A5LGp.

Catch up with favorite characters in this holiday short romance which includes spoilers. Holiday Collection here https://books2read.com/u/bzd59G.

For small-town, single mom stories, check out *Until Serena*: https://books2read.com/u/mej8vr.

Always fun when you love billionaire romances, so check in with *Cocky Catcher*, a sports romance, enemies to lovers here: https://books2read.com/u/bOxNgJ.

Some familiar characters show up in *Bossy Billionaire*, a workplace, enemies to lovers romance here: https://books2read.com/u/mvZoDq.

All curvy girl, plus size romance lovers get into *I Deserve His Love*, a standalone, second chance romance here: https://books2read.com/u/mVrGwP.

The fantasy romance readers look no further than *Red Light District*, a curvy girl, fling romance here: https://books2read.com/u/m2RQ6G.

Dark Mafia readers delve into The Carrington Cartel Series a forbidden, arranged marriage here:https://books2read.com/u/mqXare?utm_source=universal+link
Claim:https://books2read.com/u/bwyjPY

Sneak Peek: Endless Summer

Farah is excited for the new chapter in her life to start. A two weeklong vacation is the perfect way to kickoff a fabulous new job in Paris. She earned it. When she meets Vincent, she isn't interested in a relationship. She just determined to enjoy the time they have together and move on. Unfortunately, she forgot to mention that to him.

Vincent, a visiting Congressman and investor, didn't know a nice meal out would lead to meeting the most beautiful woman he's ever seen. From the moment he laid eyes on her, he knew his heart was in trouble, but he didn't let that stop him from pursuing her.

What he doesn't yet know is that their hot summer fling has a timeline. Two weeks and he'll never see or hear from Farah again. When he finds out, he does everything in his power to make sure that doesn't happen.

Heart of Stone Universe

Broken 1 Emery and Jackson

https://books2read.com/u/boWPAV

Heart of Stone Book 1.5

https://payhip.com/b/kWg7

Rebirth 2 Jordan and Damon

https://books2read.com/u/ba2OMx

Heart of Stone Book 3.5 Bottoms Up

https://payhip.com/b/HGP1

Reveal 3 Angela and Brent

https://books2read.com/u/31rx9l

Renew 4 Jessica and Joseph

https://books2read.com/u/4NXyPG

Struck of Love Universe

The Early Years-A Prequel
https://books2read.com/u/49Zjnw
Ruthless Struck In Love Book 1
https://books2read.com/u/4AxKLo
Savage Struck In Love Book 2
https://books2read.com/u/bpED6g
Beast Struck In Love Book 3
https://books2read.com/u/3LpgdJ
Janice and Carlo Captivated By His Love
https://books2read.com/u/b6je6M
Brutal Struck In Love Book 4
https://books2read.com/u/4NQyE9
Stolen-Fuertes Mafia Cartel Book 1
https://books2read.com/u/mvZlgV
Saved-Fuertes Mafia Cartel Book 2
https://books2read.com/u/4DWwLd
Redemption Struck In Love Book 5
https://books2read.com/u/b5kZ8O
Betrayal- Fuertes Mafia Cartel Book 3
https://books2read.com/u/4A5LGp

Torn: The Carrington Cartel Book 1
https://books2read.com/u/mqXare?utm_source=universal+link
Claim: The Carrington Cartel Book 2
https://books2read.com/u/bwyjPY

Also By Chiquita Dennie

Series

Struck in Love

The Early Years-A Prequel Short Story
Ruthless:Antonio and Sabrina Book 1
Savage: Antonio and Sabrina Book 2
Beastl: Antonio and Sabrina Book 3
Captivated By His Love:Janice and Carlo
Brutal: Antonio and Sabrina Booke 4
Redemption: Antonio and Sabrina Book 5

Heart of Stone

Broken, Book 1 (Emery & Jackson)
A Valentine's Day Short Book 1.5 Emery & Jackson
Rebirth, Book 2 (Jordan and Damon)
Reveal, Book 3 (Angela and Brent)
Bottoms Up Book 3.5 Jessica and Joseph Short
Renew, Book 4 (Jessica and Joseph)

Cocky Billionaire Boys

Cocky Catcher (Cocky Billionaire Boys Book 1)
Bossy Billionaire (Cocky Billionaire Boys Book 2)

The Fuertes Cartel

Stolen (The Fuertes Cartel Book 1)
Saved (The Fuertes Cartel Book 2)
Betrayed (The Fuertes Cartel Book 3)

Carrington Cartel

Torn: The Carrington Cartel Book 1
Claim: The Carrington Cartel Book 2

Something

Something Gained: A Romantic Comedy Book 1
Something Earned: A Romantic Comedy Book 2

Pierce Motors

Refuel:(Pierce Motors Book l)
Pressure:(Pierce Motors Book 2)

Summer Break

Summer Nights(Summer Break Book 1)

TN Seal Security

Aydin: Book 1
Nasir: Book 2
Nicco: Book 3

Standalones

Until Serena(HEA World Novel)
Temptation
She's All I Need

I Deserve His Love
Mutual Agreement
Scoring with Sadie
Exposed (A Bodyguard Novel)
Love Shorts:A Collection of Short Stories
Red Light District(A Fantasy Romance Short)

By Keke Renée:

Wet Heat
His Peace, Her Pleasure
Baby, It's Cold Outside
Love Don't Live Here Anymore, Book 1, 2
Every Time We Touch (A Wet Heat Novelette)
One Night Only- Love By Design Book 1
Cassian and Savannah Love By Design Book 2
Deidra's Love -Love By Design Book 3
Protecting Bria: Book 1
Protecting Chanel:Book 2
Protecting Yanira: Book 3
Haven: A Single Dad Romance
Sensual
Seek to Please: Book 1
Seek To Touch: Book 2
Seek To Bare:Book 3
Seek To Love: Book 4
Seek To Trust: Book 5
Seek To Earn: Book 6
Tease Me: Book 1
Promise Me: Book 1

By Ava S.King

Fatal Memory: Book 1 Teagan Stone
Fatal Target: Book 2 Teagan Stone

Fatal Crime: Book 3 Teagan Stone
Fatal Justice: Book 4 Teagan Stone
Fatal Enemy: Book 5 Teagan Stone
Fatal Death: Book 6 Teagan Stone
Fatal Revenge: Book 7 Teagan Stone
Fatal Pursuit: Book 8 Teagan Stone
Mirror of Lies: Book 1
Mirror of Lust: Book 2
Ruined: Andi Easton Book 1

Thank you so much for reading and if you enjoyed the crazy ride and decide to leave a review we'd truly appreciate the support..

About the Author

Chiquita Dennie is an author of Contemporary, Romantic Suspense, Erotic, and Women's Fiction.

Chiquita lives in Los Angeles, CA. Before she started writing contemporary romance, she worked in the entertainment industry on notable TV shows such as the Dr. Phil show, the Tyra Banks show, American Idol, and Deal or No Deal. But her favorite job is the one she's now doing: full-time writing romance.

A best-selling author and award-winning filmmaker, her first short film, "Invisible," was released in summer 2017 and screened in multiple festivals and won for Best Short Film. She also hosts a podcast that showcases the latest in beauty, business, and community called "Moscato and Tea." Her debut release of *Antonio and Sabrina Struck in Love* has opened a new avenue of writing that she loves. Nominated for 2021 Author of the Year, Best Black Romance "Mutual Agreement," and Best Interracial Romance for "She's All In Need". In 2022 nominated Author Queen of the Year, Best Black Romance "Nasir" Best Interracial Romance "Torn" and Best Romantic Comedy "Something Gained" by Black Girls Who Write.

If you want to know when the next book will come out, please visit my website at http://www.chiquitadennie.com, where you can sign up to receive an email for my next release.

What's Next?

Want to know what happens next?

Follow me on social media to catch the next release.

Reviews are the lifeblood of the publishing world. They're read, appreciated, and needed. Please consider taking the time to leave a few words on Goodreads, or bookbub.

Sign up for updates and sneak peaks at the site below.

https://www.bookbub.com/chiquitadennie

https://www.chiquitadennie.com

https://www.goodreads.com/author/chiquitadennie

https://Facebook.com/chiquitassteamyreadinggroup

x.com/authorchiquitad

https://www.instagram.com/authorchiquitadennie

https://www.Facebook.com/authorchiquitadennie

https://www.304publishing.tumblr.com

304 Publishing Company

We showcase authors writing Romance, Women's Fiction, Thriller, and Erotic.Along with Mystery, Suspense, Poetry, Beauty, and Style Books. Thank you for taking the time out to visit. Join our mailing list to stay updated with new releases and blog posts.

Acknowledgments

I want to dedicate this to my team that helps me behind the scenes, from my editors, test readers, graphic designers, and the list goes on.

Truly appreciate each of you for keeping me on my toes.

Milton Keynes UK
Ingram Content Group UK Ltd.
UKHW042146150524
442688UK00001B/25

9 781955 233705